RUNAWAY BRIDE

Della Donovan loved Max—she was sure of
that—and she would be his wife in six weeks.

But why did the thought of marriage terrify
her? The usually happily hectic days of
wedding preparations merely set Della to
trembling with fear . . . a fear that could
ruin her love—her marriage—her life . . .

Escape From Love

A love story by

Betty Blocklinger

Published by
MODERN PROMOTIONS
A Division of Unisystems Inc.
New York, N.Y.

1

"AND THIS," Lottie's voice trilled softly, "is the apartment I had made up for Max and Della."

Across the hall Della Donovan heard the voice, stiffened and clamped her hands to the arms of the chair.

"It is charming," cried the visitor. "Those lucky young people!"

Della's nails scratched the wood. Lucky! Why couldn't she admit it? She must think of the weeks of care, money and effort Lottie had expended on the three rooms of the old Donovan house, Lottie's by the terms of their father's will, and be grateful.

Lottie's voice came again. "Max is a fine young man, but naturally he hasn't had time to get lucrative returns from his profession."

She would close the door and lock it, thought Della frantically. She couldn't listen to any more of this. Lock it? Lottie didn't believe in locks on inside doors.

"Yes, the wedding is next week. What? Oh, pink."

Della shuddered. Rough pink-textured covering for

divan and chairs; deeper pink for the rug. Bath and kitchen a mass of pink ruffles, and pink soap dishes; a pink bedroom.

And her wedding! How could she walk down the church aisle with each pew flanked by pink blossoms; be followed by bridesmaids in every shade of pink; return to a reception where even the wedding cake was iced in pink?

"I can't," she whispered. "I can't marry Max."

The strange sickness was striking again. She felt as though her body were strung with wires and plugged into some high voltage circuit. A moment of this; then dizziness and nausea.

"Della, what's wrong?"

It took her a moment to identify the girl at the door as her closest friend, Ruth Brewer, and still another to answer.

"I don't know," she whispered. "It's that dreadful feeling I've been having. Dr. Ken has given me every known test. He insists I'm in perfect health, yet—"

"Perfect physical health," mused Ruth. "Della, you're not subconsciously trying to be ill to escape marrying Max?"

"Oh, no!" There was strength to her denial. "I love Max, and goodness knows that love has been put to the test these past three years. You remember how Lottie felt about him; not that she was ever cruel in her criticism—"

"I know; just rational. She didn't want you to marry too young."

"Oh, but that's over. Now they get along beautifully. Why, Max even sides with her against me at times."

"Then is it moving into the apartment instead of into a place of your own?"

"Oh, but it is my own. I mean Father left the

property the way he did to protect Laura and me.
Lottie was older and had been married."

Again Lottie's voice came gentle, wistful. "With
Laura making that dreadful marriage so soon after
my husband lost his life, it leaves just Della and me.
She's become that much more precious to me."

Quietly Ruth turned back and closed the door.
How well she remembered radio, television and
newspapers blaring the story of the light plane over-
due, the futile search, the belief that Earl Cross had
overshot the coast line and come down in the Pacific.
But he hadn't. A year later the plane wreckage was
found in the Siskiyous, far off course. It was assumed Cross had attempted to bail out and that some
day a cattleman on summer range or some hunter
would stumble upon his remains.

"You see why Max and I have to start here, don't
you?" Della asked eagerly.

Ruth came to a sudden decision. "I'm running into
the city. Why not come along for the drive? No,
don't tell Lottie; I will. Here." she skewered a knit
skull cap over the dark curls, slipped lax arms into
a topcoat. "On your way."

Ruth came out of the house on the run, jumped
into the car and shot it into the street. "Here we
go," she said brightly.

"Ever hear from Laura?" she asked conversa-
tionally as they left town and sped out on the freeway.

"Not directly. She called me from San Francisco,
but it was a collect call and the phone is in Lottie's
name. Lottie wouldn't accept the call unless Laura
talked to her. You do undertand Lottie was protecting me, don't you?"

Ruth didn't and said so.

"We think she needed money, and Lottie believed
she was better able to supply it. But Laura wouldn't

talk to her. I'm worried. I tried to get her address from the bank, but they said they weren't free to divulge it. You know, of course, we all have a small annuity from the estate."

Ruth nodded. The whole town had known about Donovan's will.

"Ruth," Della's voice was hoarse, "I can't marry Max. It's these strange spells I have. Our marriage wouldn't have a chance. They're so frightening, and I can't explain."

"I know," her friend soothed her. "I don't understand them, but I'm taking you to someone who will. A wonderful man, a doctor who uses psychiatry as much as he does medicine."

"You don't think my mind—"

"Don't be a dope. If your mind can tell your hands, feet and heart what to do, it can squeeze nerves, can't it? And you are terribly nervous for some reason. Just trust me."

"You mean there is someone who might help?"

Ruth's laugh was hearty. "Sweetie, a rare disease is so rare you rarely hear of it. Dr. Ken's an old darling, but he hasn't all of the answers. Let's try my Dr. Dan."

Della was ready to try anything.

For a moment she thought Ruth might be taking her to some quack, but when they drove up before a medical building she was reassured.

She sat in a comfortable straight-backed chair while Ruth's "Dr. Dan" answered a telephone call.

At first there was only friendly conversation. Later she told him of the peculiar seizures she had had, and he nodded.

"Quite usual, though ordinarily farmers and big businessmen complain. We can relieve this nerve tension."

"But farmers don't have nerve tension," she protested.

"Miss Donovan, can you think of a more formidable opponent than the weather? Consider the man whose livelihood for his family depends upon something over which he has no control; picture anything more frustrating."

But she was neither a farmer nor a businessman or woman. She had everything and said so. She came of a good small city family, had a nice home, was about to marry the man she dearly loved. The only other person close to her was her sister, who was so good, so gentle and kindly everyone in the city looked upon her as the epitome of fine womanhood.

"Does she ask you to follow whatever current diet she is following?" he asked.

"Yes." Della laughed a little. "And she does follow any that anyone suggests. How did you know?"

They discussed Max, and Della glowed. She'd admired him when she was a freshman in high school and he a senior. Then he'd gone away to college and to law school, and she'd seen him only occasionally during his brief vacations, from a distance.

Not until he had been taken into a local firm and she'd met him at a mutual friend's had they become really acquainted. At that it had taken her a long time to win her sister over to accepting their engagement.

"But I can't marry him," she concluded, and sank back, the familiar tremor coursing through her body.

"Not yet," he agreed, smiling.

He gave her a small white pellet to take; then went on easily, "We can relieve this condition; the cure lies within you. You are like the farmer in conflict with the weather; except that you haven't identified your opponent.

"Remember the biblical quotation: 'Agree with

thine adversary lest he have his way with thee.' That means coming to an understanding. That is what you must do. First identify your adversary; then understand him, come to terms with him. Believe me, those terms will benefit both of you."

Half an hour later Della wafted into the reception room, let Ruth guide her out to the parking lot, then sat puzzled.

"Any place you want to go before we start home?" Ruth asked.

"Drugstore. A prescription. Ruth, of all things, a tablet of airplane paper, a large metal ash tray and book matches. Is he crazy or am I?"

"We're all a little, aren't we? How do you feel?"

"Relieved," Della replied promptly. "At learning there are thousands walking around with this disease. He's going to call Dr. Ken and suggest he ask the wedding be postponed until I've conquered this whatever it is."

"Extreme hypertension," Ruth said; then quickly, "Della, I lied to him. I told him you'd had a fainting spell while we were shopping. Otherwise he couldn't have taken you. He'll be explaining that to Dr. Ken, so don't let me down."

"You mean you talked to him before—"

"I drove to the city on purpose so I could phone. Then I went back to pick you up if I had to hit both you and Lottie over the heads and drag you off by your hair. Any time a gal like you hits the skids as you have since I've been away, it calls for drastic action. Believe me, one doesn't just walk into his office and find him waiting with open door."

They made their purchases and drove out of the city before Della returned to the subject. "Ruth, do you know what is causing my condition?"

"I think I do. I imagine now Dr. Dan really knows. But if either of us were to tell you, you'd have another conflict added to the ones you already have."

"But, Ruth, think of the time I'd save. This way I can't marry Max until I know and am well again."

"Della, this way, when you know, the knowledge will come from within you and carry the deep conviction you have to have. If either one of us breathed a hint, your defense mechanism would rear up and blame us for coloring your thoughts. Now be happy."

Della relaxed and looked out of the car windows. Far to the west reared the coast range, Dutch blue in the late afternoon. Nearby fields were being ploughed; hedgerows were a new green.

A meadowlark swinging on a bough lifted with a flash of white on his underwings, singing his joy in the spring of the year, and Della's spirits lifted with the song. She had a chance, a new, freshly given chance to be happy again.

"Hm," muttered Ruth. "I'd better find a gas station; forgot to check before we started out."

The county seat lay just ahead. There were many gas stations, but by then Ruth wasn't being choosy. Her car needed immediate attention, and that would be obtained at a place on the right where great diesel trucks loomed high, dwarfing the buildings.

"Want to get the kinks out?" Ruth asked. "Everybody here seems concentrating on that refrigerator truck."

Everybody was. The big truck with its load of perishables had a broken line; if it were not fixed soon there would be defrosting and a loss of cargo.

Nearby was a logging truck; the driver was leaning against the cab step.

"From Skyhigh," he was telling a questioner.

Skyhigh had been Lottie's husband's favorite hunting center. Instantly a memory flashed into Della's mind: Earl sitting in a deep chair, wistful eyes on the fireplace flames, telling all who'd listen about that little ghost town lost in the clouds of the coast range.

Dimly the memory of Lottie's words came: "Well, dear, if you enjoy being lost in the clouds, why not plan to spend more time there?"

Why hadn't he? Della stood frowning, trying to recall a particular trip Earl had planned there. Then something had happened. Oh, yes, Earl's favorite cousin had arrived unexpectedly.

She was feeling ill again.

"Are you all right, miss?"

Della shook her head to clear her vision. The log truck driver was beside her, bracing her.

"I'm sorry," she faltered. "It was the name Sky-high. I heard you mention it. A relative who was killed loved the place."

He nodded sagely. "Some do and some don't. Those of us who do count any time away from there lost."

"Lost! He said it was lost in the clouds."

"At times, when the mist rises or when the coast fog rides in to fill the valleys. But we're above the mist and the fog; we have sunlight and starlight when the rest of the world lies heavy under a cloud."

Della looked around. Ruth was talking to an attendant, and the man was walking her back to the car. "Better sit down," he'd said.

She wanted to. Yet she wanted to keep on talking to this man, hold him there by conversation.

"Is it far? Is it hard to reach?"

"Well," he qualified, "it isn't a place people go for a Sunday afternoon drive. But there's a good hard-top road all the way and not much traffic. Half the houses in town are for rent or for sale."

Ruth came up, apologizing. "I had literally to tear that attendant off the truck," she complained, "and all he was doing was looking."

A moment later they were under way; Della responded to the log truck driver's salute with a wave.

"My word, what a handsome man!" Ruth cried. "If I weren't married—"

"He was?" Della turned and looked back. An ell of the building cut him from view, and she shrugged. It didn't matter. She'd never see him again.

2

LOTTIE was near the doorway when Della entered.

"Did you have a nice time?" she asked eagerly. "I wanted to join you! I've some last minute shopping to do. But," she shrugged and smiled, "Ruth was in such a hurry she didn't hear what I said.

"Oh?" She glanced at the packages Della carried. "You shopped. What did you buy?"

Della's hands tightened convulsively on the larger package. How could she possibly explain an ash tray to Lottie?

"Just something," she murmured.

"A gift for me," surmised Lottie happily, and from Della's now nerveless fingers the package slipped to bounce on the hardwood floor.

"Della, not an ash tray! Della, you're not taking up smoking? Darling, I don't think Ruth is quite—"

"I am not taking up smoking," Della managed stonily.

"Then Max is? Oh, I'm sorry. There's such an odor. Ed never smoked in the house. He seemed to sense how I felt."

"Father smoked," Della reminded her.

"Yes, and it hastened his demise."

"Grandpa, who had a pipe so strong it walked out and met him at the door, lived to be ninety-four. Do you remember what he said when he decided to die? That he was tired of this world and wanted to try a new one."

And she thought: I, too, am tired of this world.

She started for the stairway. Lottie's gentle voice reminded her dinner was ready and that she had tried to prepare something Della would eat.

It took her four hours to free herself from Lottie's concern. Max had telephoned early, before going to some political dinner, and Della hung up wondering if she had sounded as uninterested as she felt. She was truly letting him down in so many ways.

Eventually, leaving her sister before the television set, she fled to her room and to the pad of paper which was to be open seasame to the cavern of her subconscious.

A rap at the door. It opened and Lottie entered. "Oh, catching up on your correspondence? Della, I am worried about you. You've acted so strangely ever since Ruth returned."

"Please." Her breath was caught, her heart pounding until it seemed Lottie must hear it.

"I thought we might talk it out."

"Trot along and get your beauty sleep," Della managed in a light tone. "Not that you need it, but we can't have the matron of honor looking exhausted."

There, she had lied again, added another lie to the hundreds of lies she'd been telling lately.

She'd take her tiny pencil flash, tent the bed covers, write there as Dr. Dan had suggested she write, even write the loathsome words that had come to her lips as Lottie talked.

But first she must feign sleep. Lottie would come in to check her breathing.

Ah, the ritual was over. Now, a chair under the doorknob.

In bed, the tiny eye of light traversed the page. At first timorously, then savagely, Della wrote. Time and again she stopped, horrified. This wasn't like her. These words, these thoughts that boiled up and spilled over like fire and again like acid—surely they were not coming from her.

How cruel they were.

Exhausted, Della flicked off the pencil flash and leaned back.

Dr. Dan had said she would find the cause of her inner conflict. She had. She, the quiet, well mannered Della Donovan, was a veritable volcano of hatred and resentment; all repressed, all boiling, seeking a means of escape.

A fresh thought struck. She must burn this paper immediately. What should she do with the ash? What if Lottie caught a whiff of burning paper and sought its source?

The old sickness struck, but it no longer frightened her. Now she stood off and analyzed it. She must take the first step in her cure.

Deliberately she fluffed the sheer sheets of paper, placed them in the ash tray and lighted them, then covered the tray until the flame died down. The ashes went out the window opening onto the driveway on the opposite side from Lottie's room. Now some facial cream to wipe out the tray.

She slept to a dream of being encased in pink plastic and awakened to find Lottie standing over her, shaking her.

Lottie talked to Dr. Ken early, before he set out on house and hospital calls; it prepared him for a

call from the city from one Dr. Daniel Kenard. Later
he talked it over with his wife.

"Mabel, exactly what do you think of the Dono-
vans? Now take Lottie. There, in my estimation, is
the best, the most even-tempered gracious woman
I've ever known."

Mabel's eyes twinkled. "Admitting I have a temper,
Kenneth? Yes, Lottie is unusual. Heaven knows I've
tried to find a flaw in her; but I haven't succeeded."

"And Della?"

Mabel hesitated. "Della has changed a great deal
in the last couple of years. She is too quiet. She is—
well, grey."

Lottie made the office call alone, for the simple
reason that Della had disappeared. When Lottie
called her for lunch she wasn't there, but there was
a note. "Please understand," Della had written, "I
have to work out a problem and need to be alone."

Lottie called Max from the doctor's office and, on
meeting him at a nearby coffee shop, gave a dis-
tressed report.

"Max, I can't understand what is happening. Dr.
Ken says Della is heading for a nervous breakdown,
but he doesn't know why. And I can't for the life of
me think of a single reason."

"Except me," Max interposed heavily.

"Oh, I can't believe that. She loves you, Max. I
know Della."

She explained the doctor's order that the wedding
be postponed until Della had had a little time at
the seashore. She didn't know how she was going to
reach everyone; she'd have to hire a secretary.

Max said one of the office underlings would probably be glad to earn the extra money, and of course
he'd take care of the financial end. Somehow he felt
he was to blame.

"Take her to the coast tomorrow, will you, Max?

I'll fix up a fine lunch. Then you oversee her choice of a place to stay. Dr. Ken intimated she should be alone, but be sure there are other people near her in case she needs them."

Moodily he nodded. He'd be over that evening.

"Oh, I wouldn't, Max." There was alarm in Lottie's voice and eyes. "Dr. Ken said rest was imperative."

When Della came in she was braced for an inquisition. Lottie would fire a barrage of gentle questions at her, and she would have to fend them off, nerve tension mounting with every question.

"Be ready for dinner soon, dear?" Lottie greeted her. "Then I'll serve in five minutes."

Five minutes' grace, thought Della, and hastened to rid herself of topcoat and hat, to brush her dark hair, to dab a little more rouge on her cheeks to offset Lottie's anxious, "You look pale; we should try another tonic."

All through dinner Della waited for the questions, but they didn't come. Waiting for them was more devastating than fending them off.

"I'm not hungry," she said at length. "Max and I will be stopping somewhere."

"Oh, I didn't tell you. Max isn't free this evening, but he'll come by early tomorrow to take you to the coast for the day."

"Why?" demanded Della bluntly.

"Dr. Ken got in touch with me this afternoon. Some city doctor who attended you the day you had the fainting spell called him. He suggested a rest at the beach for a couple of weeks. Max will take you down to find a hotel or apartment."

"And the wedding?"

"Oh, that." Lightly Lottie waved a hand. "Max was able to put off his vacation, it being so early in the spring, so we'll send out notices of a postponement. No one will be surprised; so many have men-

tioned how poorly you've looked since your bout with
the flu last winter. Now run along and rest; I'll do
the dishes."

Della didn't run. With an effort she mounted the
carpeted stairway, hoping to reach her room before
waves of illness forced her to sit down. She had capsules in her handbag. She had paper and pencil,
ash tray and matches. She had to force this poison
out of herself.

She couldn't write anything tonight. She'd take
a tablet and go to bed, try to look less like a hag the
next morning.

She awakened happy, dressed with a song on her
lips and, when Max came, leaned from the window
to wave down at him.

"Isn't this a glorious day?" she sang out.

"As beautiful as you look to me," he returned
soberly.

She waited a moment, feeling love like gossamer
thread binding them, then hurried for a heavy topcoat and cap and walking shoes to be tossed into the
car.

Lottie, looking flushed and happy, had a huge ham-
per ready. "I thought it would be more fun for you
to picnic on the beach. It's such a lovely day."

The chicken, she told them, was fresh fried; she'd
been up since before daybreak. And she'd baked
little individual pies. Had they ever taken that road
to the coast between Neskowin and the Otis cut-off?
It was private, and delightful.

She came out to the car to make sure Della hadn't
forgotten rugs and then ran back for a large thermos
of water, should they want more coffee than she'd
provided.

Soberly they watched. She was like a child preparing a party for somebody else.

"Oh, what the deuce," grumbled Max as she returned. "Lottie, there's always room for one more. Why not pop in and go with us?"

She said she couldn't, then with a great sigh murmured, "You just don't know what it would mean to me," and in almost no time had crowded in beside Della.

"Let's go by the northern route and come back by the southern," she suggested.

They took Sunset Boulevard, the northern cross-valley freeway, but Della hardly saw it. Her handbag had been tossed to the back of the car. In it were the capsules she needed so dreadfully, for she was ill again.

They started upgrade to look down on what Max called adolescent mountains, to look out on great ranges stretched against the western sky.

Della made no effort to join the conversation. She'd concentrate upon the landscape. Crossroad, county roads, and ahead a single sign. She saw it as they flashed past—Skyhigh.

They took the private road Lottie suggested and came out on a beautiful beach. After lunch, which Della made only a pretense of eating, Lottie withdrew to sit staring out at the surf.

"Della," Max took the lax hand lying beside him, "are you upset because I asked Lottie to join us?"

"I'm not that selfish," she said wearily. "Lottie has had so few pleasures since Earl's death. A widow her age doesn't fit into groups. It's just this—"

"I know." He patted her hand. "Lottie told me what Dr. Ken explained to her. Now let's go shopping for that apartment. Or would you prefer a hotel?"

"Not many open this early, and I would prefer an apartment. I want to get up when I want to, eat what I want, be completely selfish."

Lottie was dubious about the apartment Della

chose. It was in an old building on a point; waves washed in at its feet during high tide. It would be windy.

"Frankly, I'll be bored if we have nothing but the sea for company," Lottie warned.

Della stiffened and swallowed. "But, Lottie, I'm to be here alone."

"Max, listen to her. Imagine me letting that poor sick child stay down here among strangers, alone. Why, Della, I wouldn't be able to live with myself."

3

MAX took a quick look at Della, then made a suggestion. "Why don't you take a front apartment, Lottie, and let Della have this one in the rear? You want people; she badly needs rest."

It would be something, Della thought. There was a door at the bottom of the rear stairs that locked. She could reach the beach, get away occasionally.

It was a compromise, but hadn't she read everything in life was a compromise? She had wanted a home of her own with Max. They were compromising on an apartment in Lottie's home, but that was better than losing Max or crucifying Lottie.

There was little talk on the drive home. Max promised to come down weekends. He told Della gravely she must spend every possible moment relaxing.

Lottie said they couldn't leave for a day or two; naturally she had to attend to any number of duties in connection with postponing the wedding.

Della said nothing. She was leaving the following

norning for the coast. Lottie could take a cab to the
depot, a bus to the coast. She had to get away.

She went back to the car with Max when he left
and stood a moment. "Try to understand," she
pleaded. "I don't yet, but the doctors tell me I will
soon."

"Don't worry, darling; I already do. Nerves are
miserable things. Just so it isn't," he hesitated, "another man."

"Max Meyer, whatever gave you that idea?" Della
flared. "You know there's never been anyone else.
Of course I dated in high school and later when you
didn't know I was around. But oh, Max, believe me,
it's you I love."

"So we take it from there. Now get well." Aware
of Lottie hovering anxiously, waiting for the sick little sister to be put to bed, he gave her a light kiss and
started backing the car from the drive.

Della slept, to awaken with a drugged, dragged out
feeling. The house was too quiet. She remembered
dimly having heard a car and voices; now she saw a
note had been slipped under her door.

She crept toward it and took it back to bed and
was glad she was there.

"Darling," Lottie had written, "I didn't tell
you last night, because I wanted you to have a
good sleep. Remember when I returned to the
landlord of the apartment house? He'd motioned
me back. We can't have those apartments, because they're closing the place to decorate for
the summer season."

"Now don't feel badly. You and I will run
down and find a nice hotel. I'm off to a com-
mittee meeting and luncheon; you'll find everything ready for breakfast and lunch. Take care
of yourself, little sister."

Half an hour later Della drove off, her overnight bag beside her. She would return only when she had found a place Lottie couldn't control, a place where she could be alone.

At noon, remembering she had had no food, she pulled into a small coast highway coffee stand. She'd taken the middle road this time, the one they hadn't traveled Sunday.

"You wouldn't know of a small cottage around here I could buy, would you?" she asked. "An inexpensive one," she added, trying to compute the money she had in the bank.

"Might," the counterman said. "Waitress who works here weekends has one she wants to get rid of. Belonged to her aunt. Aunt's gone to live with her kids. Ain't much of a place, but with fixin' it wouldn't be bad at all."

Later Della stood before the cottage and admitted it "wasn't much." Yet it had a certain coziness.

When she turned from opening the door, she saw the small sheltered porch looked out across sand dunes, with a V of the Pacific showing.

Slowly she entered. The furniture was old and worn. Slipcovers would fix that. She could paint the walls. It would give her something to do. The kitchen was the best room in the house, with a huge old wood stove, and an electric plate to one side.

Back through the house she moved, estimating, redressing, redecorating. She would buy it; then she and Max would have something of their very own, a place to go weekends. They could even use it for a honeymoon cottage instead of taking an aimless drive through the southern part of the state.

"Interested in buyin'?" asked an old voice.

"I may be." Della smiled at the wiry little woman who'd come around the house.

"Don't look the type for wild parties. You'll do.

We're clannish around here. Like to be left to ourselves but like neighbors handy in case of emergency.
You alone?"

Della explained that she had been ill and noticed
she wasn't queried about the illness. The doctor had
suggested a place at the shore where she could recu-
perate before marrying. She thought the cottage
would be ideal for a weekend place after that; her
husband-to-be was a lawyer.

"Good. Now make a list; things are hard to come
by down here until the season opens."

Happily Della complied, then returned to the roadside stand to find the owner had located the waitress.
All they needed was a real estate form and they'd
be on their way.

They discussed terms. Della had only fifty dollars
with her. "My sister feels I'll be more careful about
spending if I keep my money in a savings account,"
she explained apologetically. "But we can use this for
earnest money."

The waitress said she'd have a cousin bring her
aunt up for the weekend. As the banks were closed
Saturdays, they could meet at her aunt's bank on
Monday, if that were agreeable. Meanwhile Della was
to keep the key and use the house if she wanted to.

Happily Della drove home, mentally computing
savings and income. She'd spent quite a bit on her
trousseau and on drapes and linens for the apartment, but she had well over two thousand in savings.

She'd worked as a private secretary until her sister
said she should stop fully to enjoy pre-nuptial parties.
Of course she owned her car. She paid Lottie seventy-
five a month as her share of food and utilities. Her
annuity from her father's estate was a hundred and
fifty.

If I pay eighteen hundred for the cottage, she
mused, that won't leave too much for decorating. But

I'll use part of each monthly annuity, and of course Max will want to do some work for the sheer fun of it.

Trees danced along the middle highway; water cascaded down, glinting in the sunlight. Life was wonderful, and that was how she felt.

An anxious Lottie awaited her. "You didn't leave a note."

"Darling, wonderful news. I was determined to find a place that couldn't be redecorated or re-rented out from under us. I," she paused dramatically, "bought a beach cottage."

"You what?"

"Bought a cottage that looks awful but is wonderful. You'll love it when we get it fixed up."

What a wonderful sister, thought Della. Imagine ever doubting her! How her face had lighted up.

"Oh, what fun! When can I see it? How much did you pay? We've worlds of things here we can take down."

She telephoned Max. Both Della and Lottie talked to him. Max couldn't get away, but they'd go down that weekend; he'd even arrange to stay over to "see the papers through" on Monday.

"You sound like yourself again, Della," he commented happily. "We'll have a time down there. Near the beach? Surf fishing, clam digging—they'll get the nerve knots untied when I'm on a tough case."

Della and Lottie drove down the next day, and Lottie found assets Della hadn't dreamed existed.

"Gray with pink trim," said Lottie, "and a pink door. Can't you just see it?"

Della shook off the warning of nerves. "Gray with a sea-green trim. Remember, this is my cottage."

"Of course, and you do it your way. Meanwhile,

I'm starved. Do we lunch at your famous roadside counter?"

They did, and Lottie met the "middle man" and the waitress. She charmed them both and learned more about them over one hamburger than Della would have learned in a month.

"Nice people," said Lottie as they started home. "Della, why don't you turn that storage room into an extra bedroom? We have some bunk beds some place. Then Max could bring me down weekends, and he could visit with you."

Della smiled happily. That would solve a problem. Imagine Lottie thinking of it.

Back in town, they browsed through the house, choosing odd pieces of furniture that could be spared and used to better advantage at the beach. Then Lottie yawned and said sea air always made her sleepy, and Della admitted she was so relaxed she could sleep standing up.

"Let's have a cup of chocolate and really let go," suggested Lottie. "I'll bring it in when I come up."

A faint tremor struck Della. She analyzed it and nodded. Hot chocolate was Lottie's panacea for everything. Della had sipped oceans of it against her will.

Well, she'd let Lottie think she had drunk this.

She took a few sips when Lottie brought it in, then said she must get the cream off her face. Besides, it was a little hot.

At the dressing table she faced herself accusingly. That chocolate had tasted queer; what was it? Ah, Lottie's naturopathic sleeping pills.

Carefully she emptied the cup and in the bottom saw a few pink granules. Now why had Lottie thought she needed them, when she had spoken of being so relaxed?

Again she sat before the mirror and really saw

herself for the first time in weeks: the strained look around her eyes, the dryness of her hair and the peculiar color of her skin.

Have to get away, she told her mirrored reflection, until I can rid myself of these weird ideas; stop hating Lottie. She's so good I must be a monster in the making ever to question her.

She'd pretend to be asleep. Lottie would come in to check.

Della lay breathing softly when Lottie entered. After she'd tiptoed out, carefully closing the door, Della sat up.

The cottage now seemed a haven, a place to which she and Max could run.

Della grew alert. Tires on the driveway. Of course people did drive their cars in to turn around, but never up the steep incline. And this had stopped. The motor had been turned off, yet there was no car door opening and closing.

Curious, Della crept from bed and looked down. Max's car, and Max was sitting there alone. She'd call.

Before she could, a figure came from the house—Lottie.

"Max," Lottie whispered. "Forgive me for calling you at this hour, but I had to talk to you, about Della and that ridiculous house she's trying to buy."

"You sounded enthusiastic enough on the phone," he objected.

"Sh, not so loud. She took a sleeping tablet, but she may not be sound asleep yet. Max, I had to sound that way. Della is in such a mental state these days she deliberately opposes anything I suggest.

"Now we must work out some plan to keep her from buying it without her being aware we are involved in any way."

Della sank to her knees, then sat leaning against

the low window. She had taken that tablet, and this was a horrible dream.

"I don't like doing things that way, Lottie. Let's bring it out in the open. I'll talk to her."

"Max, it won't do any good. Son, don't you realize I love my little sister more than anything in the world? I want nothing but what is good for her. That's why I made you two wait so long. I had to be sure you were right for each other. Max—"

Della didn't know whether Lottie's voice had dropped or whether her mind refused to listen further. The next words she heard alerted her.

"Good. We'll plan a delaying action. I'm convinced she'll become sick of the place when she has time to think it over."

Max asked if that were fair to the present owner, and Lottie considered this. "No, it isn't, is it? I'll tell you what I'll do. I'll write you a check in full; then you run down and buy the place in my name. I'm sure after a little painting and papering I can sell at a profit when the season opens. That is," she added, "if Della is sensible by then, which she will be."

He reminded her Della had paid earnest money on the place, and Lottie said she could get around that. She'd met the niece of the owner. She would tell her she was buying it as a gift for Della, a wedding present.

Max said something, and Lottie chided him gently. "Stop being so independent. After all, who have I but you two now that Earl—" her voice broke "—is gone? And I can visit down there with you weekends."

Sickness such as she had never known struck at Della. Now she was remembering something about Earl and that trip he'd planned to Skyhigh. Lottie had worked behind the scenes to check him. She had

telephoned an urgent invitation to those cousins; had
paid their travel expenses.

Other memories crowded in. She thought of her
father's plans, his original will. Lottie had caught
Laura in some extreme misbehavior. Laura had
sworn she was not guilty. She had said it was like
a stage set, and she'd been pushed onto it. Yet the
will had been changed.

And I didn't believe her, Della mourned.

Laura, Della how knew, wouldn't have eloped
had she not been seeking a way out of an impossible
situation.

If I knew where she was I'd join her.

The car motor had started. Lottie's voice rose a
little. "Oh, the neighbors aren't bad, though there
was one man I questioned—a blond Viking type, an
artist batching in a veritable hut."

Della had seen no blond Viking.

Now came Max's voice. "I hope you're right about
this, Lottie. I'll play along until Della's out of the
rest home."

Max, who knew her, believed she needed to go into
a rest home. Lottie could influence him to that extent. And he would work with her sister to keep her
from having the beach cottage; from having something of her very own.

A new quality was born in Della at that moment;
a cunning such as comes to those who are trapped.
Ill and heartbroken as she felt, she crept into bed
again to feign deep slumber.

This was not the time to fight with Lottie. Something told her she couldn't win, not yet. She must
have time to digest this disillusionment; time to
care what happened, for at the moment she didn't.

Gradually, as the night wore on, Della's mind
cleared. One thought stood out. Max didn't believe
in her; she could no longer depend upon Max.

The sky was faintly pink outside her window when lethargy, rather than peace, stole over her. She knew now what she must do. When she awakened, when her mind was fully alert, she would plan her escape from the love of Max and Lottie.

4

DELLA came groggily awake to the smell of coffee. Lottie stood beside the bed, a breakfast tray in her hands.

"Here, dear, sit up," she urged, Della pushed herself up. "My, I've had a time waking you," her sister went on. "All you'd do was groan."

"Took a sleeping pill last night."

As she made the remark the tray jerked and the coffee spilled. "Now see what you—oh, dear, Della, it was my fault. I didn't know you ever took anything. My goodness, this tray—I'll have to clean it."

Stonily Della waited. Lottie had thought she had taken a pill in addition to the one she'd put in the chocolate. All right, let her worry; it might teach her a lesson.

"I'm not hungry," she managed, thinking she'd never again be able to drink from any cup Lottie handed her.

"But, dear, you must eat to keep up your strength. We have so much to do today."

"What?" Della asked.

"Oh, I thought we might shop for curtain material, run up curtains to take down to the cottage."

"The way I feel right now," Della yawned, "I don't care about curtains or cottage. What I'd like is some place I could just lie in bed and have my meals brought to me. Not here," she added. "I'd worry about you climbing stairs."

"Well, then," Lottie's cheeks were as pink as the crockery on the tray, "why don't you? We could look up a hotel that caters to tired bodies. Would you like that?"

"I would like you to," Della replied honestly. "And when you find one, let's run into town for some lounging clothes. I don't want to use my trousseau."

"Wonderful. You're sure you don't want just a cup of coffee?"

Della made a grimace of distaste. "My mouth feels bitter enough as it is."

At the doorway Lottie turned back. "And the cottage?"

"We've plenty of time, haven't we? I'd like to have it, naturally, but a title search takes a little time. I'll feel better able to cope with it if I'm rested."

"Just what I thought," Lottie said happily, and hurried out.

So that was how it was done, thought Della. You didn't actually lie; you just misled.

Now to plan further deception. If she were to draw everything out of her savings account, word would get back to Lottie.

"Five hundred," she murmured, "and those bonds. I can say I'm putting some jewelry in the safe deposit box. I'll pick up another five hundred and my insurance papers. Now how can I get into the vault without having Lottie at my elbow?"

The car was her own. How far could she drive

before Lottie discovered she was gone and spread an alarm? Knowing how her sister's mind worked, she wouldn't put it past Lottie to have her pronounced mentally unfit and picked up by the first state highway patrolman to spot the car license number.

She would need a few hours driving time, a chance to get far away before her absence was discovered.

For a moment she thought of the shore cottage, then shook her head; that would be the first place they would look.

If she only had someone she could trust to help her. She had Ruth and Dr. Dan, but she could not involve them in this. She must escape alone.

Della dressed carefully, the better to refute any stories Lottie might drop gently among friends. Then, in the kitchen, while Lottie telephoned in the hall, she made instant coffee and toast.

"Oh, there you are." Lottie came in, beaming. "Darling, why must you use that awful old mug for drinking? If I didn't need it for certain measurements, I'd break it."

She had, she said, found the perfect hotel. Well, not a hotel exactly, but a convalescent home, though the patients were all ambulatory. They would have an opening the day after tomorrow.

"And it is close enough for Dr. Ken and the rest of us to drop in and visit you. Max will be greatly relieved I'm sure."

"Why?" asked Della.

"My goodness, Della, the man loves you; naturally he's noticed the change in you. It's been a tremendous worry to all of us."

"I see."

It was a hair-trigger day. At times Della felt she shouldn't be driving a car.

She was finished at the bank long before **Lottie** returned from some errand.

"Now home for a rest; then to pretty up," murmured Lottie. "Max is coming to dinner."

It was then Della had to drive to the side of the street, to sit for a moment with her head on the wheel, Lottie beside her.

"Sorry," Della apologized. "It must have been that sleeping pill I took last night. Lottie, could we have Max tomorrow night? I still feel groggy."

"Of course. And, dear, you'd better give those pills to me. Sometimes one forgets one has had a pill and takes another."

"Of course. And I won't need one tonight; I'm going to bed as soon as we reach home."

She left her car in the drive way and left her sister to unload, then went to her room to sleep, to catch up on the tortured hours of the previous night.

Lottie came, and once Max came with her. Della heard him whisper, "She looks better already; she has a little color in her face. I'm certainly glad she has you to take care of her, Lottie."

"Those dreadful pills," Lottie murmured. "I'll just leave a tray in case she wants anything."

She left the tray, and Della wisely ate from it. Later she heard Lottie come in and remove it with murmurs of satisfaction. Lottie would go to bed now, assured her good work for the day was over.

Della wrote under the covers again, pouring out her feeling to Dr. Dan.

Then she wrote a note of gratitude to Ruth for taking her to Dr. Dan. She explained that she was running away. She was sorry she hadn't been able to find Laura's address; she'd been afraid to try again at the bank.

"Should you by any chance find her, please tell her now I understand what was done to her and how sorry I am I didn't have sense enough to see her innocence at that time."

Her letter to Max was the most difficult. It was also the briefest. She told him she had not drunk the chocolate into which Lottie had slipped a pill and thus had heard their conversation in the driveway. Now that she knew he *could* work with Lottie to thwart her, marriage was out of the question. She was leaving his ring in her jewel box. Lottie would hand it to him.

"It isn't a question of love, Max, because I do love you. I suppose in a way I still love Lottie. But if I am to survive, I must escape from love."

To Lottie she wrote:

"Now that I have proof of how you work behind the scenes to gain your own ends, I want no more of you. I am going to a place where I will be safe from your kind of love. Worry if you want to, but don't try to find me. If you do I will give the newspapers a story that will let the home town folk know why Laura eloped; why I am running away; even why father left the property to you. And remember this, too, Lottie. Don't try to claim I am mentally unsound; there are better doctors than Dr. Ken who will testify I am proving my sanity by escaping from the gentle manipulation of your mind."

Now she was ready. Swiftly she dressed and from her window dropped bedding and pillows and such clothes as she had not already left in her car on her return from the shopping trip.

For a long moment she stood looking at the photograph of Max on her dressing table, then with a shake of her head turned away.

The first produce trucks were passing when Della slipped downstairs, went to the car and, releasing the brakes, let it coast into the street. Then she was on her way.

She stopped at the only overnight gas station, requested the attendant check her tires. "I'm heading for San Francisco," she said, "and there are long stretches between stations."

She drove south until out of sight, then took a dirt road across the valley and headed northwest, always seeking farm roads.

The sky turned grey, then pink. Finally, on a county road, she found a grocery store opening.

She bought breakfast supplies. Farther along, at another store, she purchased more. And at a third store, which had a small hardware section, she stocked up on cookware and dishes.

"I bought a shore cottage last week," she confided, though the man seemed uninterested. Again she headed north and again turned west on a gravel road. At a wooded spot she stopped to study the road map.

South again, then west, and there was the freeway. Della waited a moment at the stop sign. She had the weird feeling she had stepped into another dimension. There was not a car to be seen, not a sign of life anywhere.

Nor did she meet any as she drove.

She saw the sign: Skyhigh. Well off the freeway, she pulled to a turn-out to dry her hands; to drink from the thermos of coffee she had put in the car the day before.

She took the indicated sedative there, wondering if she should. That log trucker she'd met at the service station with Ruth had said the road up was not one for Sunday drivers. At this hour she could meet a log truck hurtling down with its load. Oh, well, she'd be on the inside, and calm nerves might be wiser.

There were times when she was tempted to turn around and retreat. But there was no place to turn, and with sharp curves behind her she dared not back.

Occasionally there were bursts of beauty, but if she more than glanced at them she would be risking falling into the chasms below.

And then, when she felt she must back into the cliff and await steadier nerves before going on, she came out on a plateau of sorts, with stands of young fir trees, some cleared acres, an occasional house.

Now the road dipped sharply down, and below lay a toy village. It must be; there was not a sign of life any place.

Gently Della eased her car down to a gas station. It was empty; windows stared out blindly. Grocery stores, notion shops, furniture stores—or so the legends on their windows read—all stood lifeless.

"Ghost town," Della murmured, and turned to look back up the hill.

There was a puff of smoke from the chimney of a little blue house, and there the thin spiral of another. Skyhigh, she reasoned, wasn't on daylight saving time; these householders were just arising.

She drove around a corner, and a huge building loomed ahead. At one time, she reasoned, this had been a tavern of some repute, else why the wide windows, the tables, and farther along the booths?

Della stared as she read the legend over the door. The tavern was now a grill room, grocery store, post office, library and city hall. And there was life inside.

She left her car in a clump of willows and walked in shakily. From behind the counter a middle-aged woman straightened and smiled. "You're up early; bet you're starved."

"I do believe I could eat," Della admitted.

"Here," a cup of steaming coffee was thrust at

her, "go over to that last booth and look at the view while I rustle up something. You look bushed."

Obediently Della followed directions. When she had sat down, she glanced out and couldn't believe what she saw.

Of course she had climbed a number of steps to enter the tavern, yet she hadn't realized it was on the edge of a sharp cliff and that the land dropped off on the other side. Blue shadows were rapidly being devoured by sunlight reflecting back from the mammoth range beyond.

"Kinda makes you feel little, don't it?" The woman was back, laying the service. "Did me when I came. I looked about like you then, all tired out. Was, too. Husband killed, and all his relatives right down to their hound dog moved in to tell me which way to turn. Except here. So I came this way."

"How did you hear about it?"

"Used to come up with my Bill, hunting. Folks here mind their own business. I knew I'd be given a chance to get my feet back under me. Now eat up."

Della took a few bites, then laid down her fork. She couldn't eat.

"Mind if I have breakfast with you? Nobody due in for a while."

And Della ate, bite by bite, unaware of the therapy the other woman was using, the adroit way she was diverting Della's mind from the simple act of providing her overstrained body with food.

One thing Della noticed: not a question was asked of her.

"I suppose," she ventured, "there are houses available, furnished ones?"

"For sale, for rent, furnished and unfurnished, and there's a lot of junk furniture in the old store you can buy for next to nothing. Wait; here comes a fellow who can give you a better run-down. Nice guy. Won't wake his folks messing around in the kitchen, so he comes here for breakfast.

"Hey, Jack, come over here."

Della had no warning—the high back of the booth was between them—but then, neither had he.

"Oh," said Della in unison with the log trucker who was responsible for her being at Skyhigh, "it's you."

"Well, good; you two've met. Sit down, Jack. Want the usual?"

5

THE TRUCKER spoke first. "I have the advantage," he said easily. "Now you know my name is Jack; last name's Lewin."

"I am," Della hesitated, "Ella Donald."

"And Ella has been sick. Thought so that day we met. Need a good rest; right?"

"So right," she breathed, "if I can find a place where no one will bother me."

"What does your physician say? Mind telling me his name?"

"Dr. Dan Kendall. He says it's nerve tension."

"Dr. Dan knows. He's one of the best. So we'll find you a place to live where you won't be bothered, yet be close enough to neighbors so they'll hear you scream when a bear comes knocking at your window."

"A bear?"

"Once in a blue moon, if you leave toothsome garbage lying around; also wildcats and cougars. Afraid?"

"No. I prefer them to good people who manipulate your affairs behind your back and won't let you take a breath without supervision."

"Good." He nodded as though understanding more than she had explained. "What other requirements?"

Della looked down on the vast bowl below, now green with trees bathing in sunshine. "Do you suppose I could find a view like that?"

Jack Lewin looked both amused and embarrassed. "You put me in a tough spot. The only place I know of with that view is our place, a three-room affair Dad threw up when he first moved out here, alone."

"Is it for sale?" Della asked eagerly. "I do have money of my own and an income. And I do need something of my very own."

"Think it could be arranged. Dad's thought of selling, but it's mostly hunters who want to buy. Sometimes they get gun-happy, and while he's well again, he says he just can't enjoy working outdoors thinking his hat may get shot off his head."

"And I could move right away, today?"

Lewin hesitated a moment. "Why not? I'll take you up to the folks', then get on with my load. Be back around three. Better load up on any groceries you'll need. We'd feed you, but I've an idea you wouldn't want that."

"Thank you," Della murmured.

He telephoned as she shopped, enabling her to hear every word. He could, she reasoned, have waited until she went to her car. This openness was reassuring.

"Dad? Bringing a young lady out to see you. She'd like to try out the cabin. She has the same thing you had when you came up. I have to take this load down; when I get back we'll rig up a couple of poles and put in a cowbell intercom. Meanwhile I guess you'll know what to do."

He was smiling when he turned from the wall

phone. "Dad said the best thing he can do for you is leave you alone. Ready?"

The waitress, turned grocery clerk, had suggested milk and eggs, bread and butter.

And then Della, once again apprehensive, turned, went out of the door and down to her car.

She found she had to retrace her route, go back up out of the canyon and along the plateau a few miles. Then Lewin drew off to the side, and she saw a modern ranch house, a hub for a flower and vegetable garden.

Down the main path came a tall, slender man with white hair who seemed to take over as his son took off with his load.

He smiled apologetically as he greeted her. "My wife ran down with a mop and broom as soon as Jack called. Now if you'd like to drive your car in, there's a trail of sorts leading down."

"Down?" asked Della doubtfully.

"Just a slight drop. No one can see the place from the road and come calling out of curiosity."

He got into the car with her, talking easily as she maneuvered along the rough roadway. If she felt as he had when he'd first come up, she'd prefer being left alone to being entertained. They'd rented the cottage occasionally and had used it as a guest house, so there was electricity. A rough place. However, she needn't look at the cabin; she could look out of the windows.

A plump matronly figure scurried out of the house as they drew near, paused and shook her head. "I'd hoped to be out of sight," she apologized, "but I wanted to air that mattress. Now you tuck in; everything's ready."

Mr. Lewin unloaded her car; then they left with the assurance there would be a wire strung between the two places after Jack's return. If she needed anything, at any time, day or night, she needed only to pull on the wire and an old cow bell would jangle in their kitchen. Later they could install a more modern intercom.

For a few moments after they left Della moved around aimlessly, pulling jeans and sweaters from bags and boxes; going to the little kitchenette and putting a few cans on the shelves; standing staring at nothing in particular.

Then she shook her head and looked at the little stove in the living room. Never had she seen anything more ridiculous. It appeared to have started out as a tall pot-bellied affair. Then halfway along its form had changed. It had been cut off at the waistline to carry gallantly, a flat two-lidded top, crowned temporarily with an ornate brass hat set ascrew.

Come on, crackled the fire inside. Let's laugh at what's happened to us.

Laugh at what had happened to her? She'd had her life "cut off at the pockets." Thus far she had carefully refrained from looking back. She had not even allowed herself to wonder what was taking place in her old home. She hadn't dared, for the faintest turning back brought with it an illness she couldn't afford until she had reached a destination.

Suddenly she threw herself on the unmade bed and began to cry.

The sun moved on west, peered into the south bedroom window, then tucked a warm golden blanket over the slim figure lying on the bed, and Della slept.

Jack Lewin delivered his load of logs, had a late lunch at a favorite spot, then went back to the cab of his truck to study the events of the morning.

The girl Ella had looked badly the day he'd first met her the week before. But what had happened within that week or ten days to cause such a change? She had looked twenty times worse that morning. And he was responsible for her living in his folks' cabin.

They wouldn't be legally responsible if anything happened to her, but morally they'd be in right up to their chins, he mused.

It was late before he got around to telephoning the city. He'd find some way of covering for this Ella, but he had to know just how sick she was.

It was late in the city, too, and Dr. Dan had read a certain letter that had come in the mail. He was all primed for the telephone call, mysterious as it seemed.

"My father's a patient of Geardon's," was the introduction. "If you don't mind, I won't give you my name or address just yet. It would make me feel I'm letting down a girl I met this morning who said she was a patient of yours. First name, she said, was Ella."

"Good, good. Where is she? Has she found a safe, quiet place to rest?" And then he added, "I'd as soon you didn't tell me where; just give me the details."

And Jack gave the details.

A slightly bewildered but very determined Jack Lewin went back to his truck and drove west. That fool doctor had said she couldn't have stopped at a better place. Lewin, senior, would understand her condition.

Della awakened slowly. Somewhere there were men's voices, but they were not directed at her. She shivered a little, opened her eyes and knew a moment of panic. She looked around her. At least she wasn't in a rest home.

She turned. Before her there was a west window; and beyond the small covered front porch, cloud shadows played hop scotch over mountains.

She glanced at her wrist watch. She had slept for six hours.

A mirror hung on the wall. One glance, and Della hurried to wash her face and comb her hair. She remembered now that she had cried; that was why her eyes looked out from between puffs.

"Miss Ella," said Lewin senior's voice, "I'm coming into the kitchen to hang the bell cord. Oh, and I brought you a few books. Ring any time you need us; if you don't, wait until you feel ready to come up. It took me two weeks to go out; wouldn't have then, but my appetite began picking up. Had to go to the store."

She found herself facing the older man of her own volition. "I don't know what I've done to deserve you," she said soberly, "but I am thankful for you. I promise to ring if I need anyone. Now that I know why I feel as I do—"

He chuckled. "I thought I was dying of some rare malady. Jack was in service, my business at the point where I could lose everything, so I knocked myself out trying to get things straight before I turned up my toes."

"Will I be able to laugh at this some day?"

The grey-blue eyes, so like Jack's, twinkled. "I've an idea you will, but it will be the laughter of wisdom. Wisdom is freedom; both are hard come by. Oh, by the way, if I were you I wouldn't worry about unpacking. I had the heebie-jeebies every time I tried. Then one day I found the place in order."

He said there would be milk left on her back porch early each morning, courtesy of the over-abundant Lewin cow, Morning Glory. If she needed groceries she could leave a note in the empty bottle.

And then she was alone, frightened, ready to flee again.

She'd taken no medicine since the night before.

Now she opened a can of soup, and while it heated swallowed a pill which seemed to stick in a dry throat.

She wouldn't sit at the table, "like a proper little lady." She would take a cup of the beverage to the front porch as an act of rebellion.

There was a weathered rocker there. Gingerly she sat in it and looked out on the vast amphitheater below, now rapidly filling with dull blue shadows running down from the canyons.

That was how she felt, hollow and filled with shadows, shadows she hadn't yet the courage to face. She wondered how Max and Lottie had taken her escape; what they were doing about it.

She lifted her glance, aware of something shining, and saw the sun had sifted its rays through western clouds to throw a sheen of silver on the snow-covered top of the range. There was still breathtaking beauty in the world if one could look up. Gradually she relaxed.

6

DELLA looked helplessly around the cabin. Disorder which she was too low in spirit to correct lay everywhere. She would make up her bed and, following Mr. Lewin's advice, forget what lay around her.

A rush of sound as though some mighty bird had passed overhead, and she stiffened, chill with fear; then came the patter of rain.

Outer doors bolted, she checked windows, picked up an armload of books and retreated to the bedroom. Bed made, hot pad inserted to take off the chill, she crept in to sit, eyes wide, dreading the hours ahead.

She reached for the books: one on philosophy; two on nervous tensions, the pages interlarded with case histories. Della wanted neither at the moment; she wanted her mind "switched off."

She picked up the last of the lot, British mysteries published forty-five years ago.

Now why had Mr. Lewin brought those down? Idly she opened one and read a page. What an easy pace. Here was neither horror nor shock tactics;

just the simple unraveling of a mystery in a quiet English countryside.

Della moved the hot pad to her shoulders to release the tension, propped pillows, lifted her head once to hear a squall stampeding across the low roof on spike heels, then started to read.

At eleven o'clock James Lewin came in, raincoat and hat glistening. "You can go back to sleep, Jack," he said; "she's settled down to read. Felt like a heel spying, but until we know what precipitated this, I thought it advisable to look in."

"Meaning first nights are the hardest?" Jack yawned.

"Not necessarily, but they do set a pattern. If you find ease on your first night, you're not afraid the next time."

Della awakened soon after dawn. Swiftly the wires of her nerves drew taut. She was facing another day. She opened her eyes and looked directly out upon a bowl of suds, high in the basin of mountains.

She didn't need to get up. She did not need to face gentle questions, probing questions, or gear herself to a day's program set by someone else.

Or did she? Would Lottie have ignored her warning? Could the car be seen? Might someone report her in this vicinity and she have to brace herself to fight for her freedom?

Anxiously she jumped up and went to the rear window of the cabin. She could barely see the peak of the Lewins' house. After the rain she could not see the tire tracks of her car. Someone, probably Jack, had cut fir boughs and laid them across the path.

"I don't need to get up," she marveled aloud.

But she wanted to build a fire. She needed oak lengths from the rear porch to hold it.

There she found a bottle of milk, half cream, and

a bottle of strained honey with a note tied around the top.

"Try these on your cereal," said the note. "Rest all you want; no one but Hanna the counter girl knows you're here. She'd be the last to tell anyone. She's been through it herself."

Hot cereal with cream and honey, and the substitute drink the doctor had advised temporarily. Della managed both.

Bowl and cup rinsed out, the little stove stoked and shut off, she returned to bed and the mystery.

There were times when she laid the book aside and looked out, or napped, awakening to tension until memory reminded her she was safely alone and could relax again.

Why, she thought, rebelliously once, couldn't Lottie have allowed me this peace?

There were times when her mind went spinning like a broken record, trying to recall, word for word, the letters she'd written Ruth, Dr. Dan, Lottie and Max.

How had Max taken the news of her escape? Had she been cruel and, above all, unjust?

It was then she would force herself to read, even reading aloud until the words sank into her mind, dimming the picture of Max.

Lottie pried the name of the city physician-psychiatrist out of Dr. Ken the next day. Dr. Dan might have avoided seeing her, but the name Mrs. Earl Cross had no association with any other patient to him.

Impressed by the office, the caliber of the waiting patients and finally by the doctor himself, Lottie gave an excellent performance of the grief-stricken older sister.

"If I knew where she was, knew she was in safe

hands, I could rest," she said in a gentle, pleading voice.

"How long?" he asked. "For how long would you allow her to follow her own destiny? Mrs. Cross, I do not have any idea where she is. Had you allowed her to take that apartment, or buy the shore cottage, you would have known. You didn't. Now leave her alone."

He had a visit from a police inspector later. To him he gave the history of Della's illness, and gave him her last letter to read.

"Cross, Earl Cross," mused the inspector. "Say, isn't she the widow of that fellow who flew out of here some four years ago and disappeared? You don't think this girl is going off the deep end, do you?"

"Not if she's left alone."

"Then you don't know where she is?"

"And don't want to know. I know she's in good hands, and if she is ever in need of treatment, I'll be called. Right now the best treatment she can have is solitude."

The inspector stood rubbing his brow with a blunt thumb. "Y'know, this makes me wonder. We wrote the Cross business off as an accident. Now I'm wondering if it was suicide.

"Gosh, and that Cross dame is such a gentle person, such a darned good woman, so sort of sweet."

"Umhum, so's whipped cream. But how would you like that forced down you as a steady diet?"

"Okay. You don't know, period."

Max Mayer also called that afternoon. Dr. Dan studied the name a few moments before having him admitted. He acknowledged to himself that he was curious.

He watched the slim, dark-haired young man with

worried hazel eyes approach, hold up his hand before Dan could speak and pose two questions.

"All I want to know is this. Is she all right? Is she in a safe place?"

Dr. Dan leaned back and tented his fingers. "Suppose I were to tell you where to find her, what would you do—go to her?"

"I'd borrow every cent I could lay hands on and build a steel fence no one could climb. I'd stay on the outside and see no one got over."

"Then you're satisfied at having your engagement broken?"

Max considered how to answer this, decided upon honesty and asked if the doctor would lose all respect for him if he admitted he was relieved?

"A healthy admission. Now go on. How about the future?"

"I don't know," Max replied. "I honestly don't know. From the time I was a senior in high I could see only one girl, Della. I didn't think I had a chance with a Donovan, so I went all out to prove myself worthy. Later, when I learned she felt the same way, I was in seventh heaven. And then—

"Well, by the time her sister had agreed to our marriage things had changed. Either Della had changed or I had. I kept thinking they'd change back, but they didn't. They became more so. Sometimes I wanted to snatch Della up and take off to tall timber. But most of the time I wanted to head for that tall timber alone."

"What was your immediate reaction to Della's letter?"

"Relief."

"Fine. Now, how do you feel toward Mrs. Cross?"

The Mayer brow puckered. "She's so reasonable, so rational," he defended her.

"And there speaks the legal mind." Dr. Dan stood

up. "Now suppose you go about building up your practice. Get out evenings; meet other girls. Above all, when you're feeling low, give thanks you're not trapped in that pink apartment."

Max had reached the doorway before the last words penetrated. He wheeled and stared at the doctor. "You mean she felt that way, too? Else how would you know about it? I didn't mention the place."

"Goodbye; come in any time." And Max was dismissed.

The storm held for three days, and for three days and nights Della clung tenaciously to her routine, mental and physical. She ate food she didn't particularly want to gather strength for her goal, freedom from Lottie; took the capsules Dr. Dan had given her; rested and doggedly read mysteries.

Once, seeking a delicacy she remembered buying, she faced the food cartons. It would take no time to place these on shelves, bring ease and order to the little kitchenette already cleaned by Mrs. Lewin.

A single attempt, and she felt such a wave of the old sickness she almost ran to the haven of the bed to sit, wondering at her revulsion.

Had it been Dr. Dan or Mr. Lewin who had said, "Don't be concerned at the recurrence of this sensation. At first any pressure—"

Pressure! Aghast, she sat up straight. She had not discussed the rental or purchase of this cabin. What must the Lewins think of her?

Hastily she scribbled a note to tie to the milk bottle: "Forgive me for being so self-centered. I simply took over your property without thought of payment. Thank you for your kindness in putting up with me. Also, I must pay for the wood I shall need shortly."

Jack Lewin, on his early morning chores, read

the note and sighed with relief. She was, as he put it, "coming to." As far as he was concerned, she could have cabin and wood for nothing, but his father had been adamant about that.

"Seems to me she has to have things her own way to feel secure. We'll play it that way until we're sure."

Della awakened to a world so flawless, snags of trees on the old Tilamook Burn miles away stood out like toothpicks.

Eagerly she hurried to the back porch and found the answer to her note.

"Dad says there's plenty of time to discuss the cottage. He says you'll be feeling more like yourself every day; take your time. Wood for your stove has to be specially cut into short lengths. We'll order a pick-up load for you; fellow up on Wild Cow Ridge makes his bread and salt cutting firewood. Leave six bucks in an envelope, or a check made out to Carl Elwood."

She felt better this morning. When she returned to the bedroom she found the idea of hibernating distasteful. In another moment she had slipped into new jeans and a pullover sweater and, with her tray, went out to sit at the south end of the porch, with the sun beating down on her back.

Seven hundred miles south, a private inquiry agent eased aching feet. Every post office, he soliloquized, should come equipped with benches at least. If that Mrs. Laura Moulton didn't come after her mail soon, his arches were going to flatten permanently.

Ah, there she was: good-looking, brisk, and with a definite chip on her shoulder. She took mail from the box, sifted through it and, her face alight, tore one letter open and began reading it before she walked out.

He had his car on a side street, ready to turn in

whatever direction her battered jalopy would take. And much good it did him. She drove into a steel-fenced enclosure after showing a pass card. Here was where he settled down for a full day's wait. Who but she and the office knew what shift she worked, how many hours to that shift?

Well, he had time to call his office.

His orders were explicit. They started, "Don't attempt it. Follow her home. Tomorrow we'll check and find the sister after she's gone to work."

He didn't. Laura Moulton had reported in, the letter from Della's friend Ruth burning into her mind. She visited the personnel manager, showed him part of the letter and asked for the afternoon off.

"Better take the day off," he advised. "You're in no condition for meticulous work."

Even as the agent talked to his office, Laura drove out, whispering, "The poor kid. After all of these years, she knows. Gosh, I hope she doesn't have to go through what I did."

An air-mail winged north on the next plane. She had gone to the airport to catch it. Among other things, she had written:

"Get her address out of that doctor somehow. Then tell her I'll stake her. I went hungry once. I didn't like it, so I've stashed some bonds away. They're hers. I'd love to have her down here; tell her I can support her and I'd love having her here."

Ruth tried.

"But I tell you I don't know," Dr. Dan insisted. "The call came through the office. It was long distance, and the girl who answered didn't check the source. I only know she is safe."

"Would you tell me if you knew?" Ruth asked bluntly.

Dr. Dan gave her a beautiful smile. "No," he replied. "From something said during our conversation, I know she's in a better atmosphere than even an understanding sister could provide."

He didn't know, but he had a good idea. He'd talked to Geardon immediately after the mysterious call. "What patient of yours took off to the woods to get rid of tensions and stayed there? Some man with a grown son. And don't tell me the place or the man's name."

He hadn't, but he had let slip, "A member of our foursome ten years ago."

"Could you ethically send him a prescription for a guest, name unknown? I think a tonic is indicated."

After the sputtering at the other end of the line had ceased came the offer: "I'll take you up there fishing. That way, as a fisherman, I can see the patient. And you can check with the man and, if you insist, have at least a distant view of her."

Della had her best day. She eyed the cartons as so many enemies. Seen as a whole, they were formidable, but if she slipped up on them one at a time they couldn't overpower her.

And she must put the kitchen in order.

Della stiffened on hearing a motor. Ah, the wood truck. She would hide so the man couldn't give her description to anyone.

Now he'd jumped out of the truck cab and turned. And Della stood, hands clamped over her mouth, holding back a scream.

7

DELLA'S next move was instinctive. She rushed to the bedroom, slid into the freshly made bed and pulled up the covers.

Dr. Dan hadn't told her the truth. Lottie had. She was insane. She should have submitted to the wiser, older sister and gone to a rest home, a mental institution.

"But I saw it!" she whispered. "It was a pick-up truck, a faded red truck, and he got out of it. I've never read of apparitions in color."

She jumped at the sound of a heavy load being dumped at the back of the house. Then she sat up. This apparition had sound effects, and only in England's oldest castles did ghosts make sounds.

"I imagined it was he," she murmured. "It was only someone resembling him."

She had to know. Not to know would mean hours of mental torture.

In another moment she had crept out to the kitchen to stand well back from the window and look at the man throwing short lengths of oak from the truck.

There, he had straightened, drawn a bandana from his pocket to wipe sawdust from his face. Now he looked out at the view.

"Earl Cross," whispered Della.

She watched as he piled up the wood. Of course he had changed; his hair was white. But he looked young and strong and peaceful.

Amnesia? she wondered. The plane had crashed three hundred miles south. He could have had a head injury and instinctively made his way to the place he loved, the mountain top "lost in the clouds."

She must get in touch with Lottie. Lottie and Earl had been the most devoted couple she had ever known.

Then sickness took over. All right, then she would ask Jack to get in touch with Lottie, to tell her where her missing husband could be found.

"Carl," she whispered. Not too different from Earl, spoken quickly. Elwood. Men would call him El. He would respond quickly to either Carl or El.

It sounded almost as though he had planned it.

But surely a man of Earl's stature, with a good business, a beautiful home and, above all, a devoted wife, wouldn't willfully isolate and exile himself.

But what was she doing? Hadn't she left Max?

Earl had nine years with Lottie, she reminded herself. I had four. I remember now how he changed. Of course Lottie made a success of him.

Lottie made him what he was. Lottie had been going to change Max's interest from criminal to corporation law. She had, she had confided to Della at one time, connections.

And I thought her good and wonderful.

In frantic haste she reached for pad and pencil. There was no one to see, she reminded herself. There would be no danger of being caught at this. And she could burn it in the little stove.

Words flashed across the page. In unrelenting black and white they etched a true picture of her eldest sister.

When she was through Della leaned back. I am not a monster, she decided, surprised. I've always known this, but pushed the knowledge down deep, been ashamed of it.

Ruth had known, and Dr. Dan.

She was faced with a new problem. Was Earl Cross a deliberate escapee from Lottie, or was he a true victim of amnesia?

Lottie was using every wile to collect the insurance. Suppose she did, and some hunter recognized Earl and reported the discovery at some distant time when she could not make restitution. Wasn't this a criminal offense? Unless amnesia could be proven, Earl would find himself in a worse trap.

From outside came the sound of wood chopping. Hastily Della jumped up, ran a powder pad over her face, a damp comb through her hair, and went to a window.

Jack Lewin was methodically splitting the short lengths.

Impulsively Della stepped out. "Please," she said, "I must talk to someone about something important."

Jack straightened to smile at her. "Will I do, or would you rather have Dad?"

"You," she decided, and added, "if you don't mind. I'll make coffee." She turned back into the kitchen.

They carried the coffee to the porch where sunshine defeated the chill wind, and for a little while Della sat trying to work out a method of presenting her problem.

"If you knew someone presumed to have been killed was really alive and healthy, would you feel bound to notify his family?"

"Is this family in need?"

"Oh, no, far from it. And she—that is, they are what you'd call adjusted. He's been dead four years. I mean in their minds he's been dead that long."

"I don't think you are speaking of yourself, but does your family think you are dead?"

"Not after the notes I left."

Jack was remembering their first meeting, her reaction to the name of the town: Skyhigh. She had spoken of a relative who had been killed, someone who had loved the place. As far as he and his parents knew, she had seen no one except the woman at the café.

Until, his memory reminded him, the wood had been delivered.

"How about insurance?" he asked abruptly.

"For some reason they've held off. They have three years to go."

"Then if no one is suffering, why do you feel it a duty to expose this person?"

Della shrank from the word expose. "Oh, I don't," she cried. "I worried, thinking he might be suffering from amnesia and would want to go home if he knew where it was. Only it isn't there any more."

"Any children?"

"No."

They sat in the sunshine, and Della found herself leaning back in the ancient porch rocker, relaxed.

"Willing to leave this up to me?" he asked.

She looked at his brown sturdiness, the dark eyes, the broad shoulders, and relaxed further.

"You won't—"

"I won't tell anyone," he promised. "I know the man you've referred to. I'll find out if he has amnesia; that's not difficult. Then we'll talk again. Meanwhile, dismiss him from your mind. You came up here to rest, remember? Possibly that's his reason

for being here. Dad came for the same reason, but
Mother let him go. She knew his need.

"Temporary escape of this kind is like sleep, a
time of restoration. To prolong it isn't healthy; it
leaves a feeling of guilt and fear of capture. Incidentally, you are looking better already."

"Thank you." Della released a deep sigh. "I am.
My mind was a 'house divided.' My instinct or subconscious or whatever you want to call it was telling
me one thing, and my conscious mind was telling me
I was a monster to harbor such thoughts."

"And now both minds are in accord and the conflict is gone."

He changed the subject quickly, pointing out a
huge hump on the range to the south. He spoke of
the radar station there, and Della, listening, wondered both at his knowledge and at his command of
words. She also wondered what he was doing here
"lost in the clouds" with his obvious education.

"I'm hungry," she said suddenly in surprise.

"Fine. Mother's having pot roast and dumplings."
Then, as she shrank back, "Up here we carry plate
dinners back and forth to show off. You'd make her
happy if you'd accept one. I suppose you have a spe-
cialty; you can send a recipe some day when you
get around to it."

He said he'd better get after the kindling; had she
noticed those clouds to the southwest? They'd stuck
their heads up over the mountains and liked what
they saw. Another three days of rain had been fore-
cast; did she mind?

"Curtains close me in safely," she replied.

She said she'd be up to discuss the cabin soon;
meanwhile, did his mother have a mail order catalogue? And how could she ever thank the Lewins for
what they were doing?

Sunset was spectacular, a mass of saffron and purple with shafts of lemon yellow.

Della watched it from a window to which she had pushed a small table. She was hungry. The pot roast was rich and brown, the vegetables not over-cooked. Dessert was, surprisingly, a fruit gelatin. And Mrs. Lewin had sent down a jar of cookies; "to make your bedtime milk slide down more easily," she'd written.

I feel good, Della thought when she was through and looked around the cabin. But when she started to unpack she grew ill again.

Oh, rubbish, she scolded herself. I'm sick and tired of giving in to you. Tonight I unpack if I have to crawl on my hands and knees.

She unpacked. And when she went to bed she carried with her the mail order catalogue, pad and pencil. Occasionally she laid them aside and wondered how Jack Lewin spent his evenings.

She wouldn't have rested so easily had she been able to follow him, for Jack had talked freely to his father and they had come to a decision.

"I'd go up there right away, son," Lewin advised. "Comes to me I saw something this afternoon I didn't understand. Now I'm afraid I do. I'm not much for interfering with other people's business, but this is different."

They reviewed what they knew of Carl Elwood and were surprised at how little it was. It had been rumored he had paid cash for a small tract of land a mile from the nearest neighbor. He had come in with a pick-up truck and camping supplies and tools.

Later he had bought a building that was about to be wrecked, had torn it down, carried the lumber to his hill and set it up again. He didn't encourage visitors, but one winter after a heavy snow some neighbors had worried about him and worked their way in.

"There he sat, baby bobcat on his knee, walls plastered with books. Had a fawn out in a little corral; said some hunter had killed the doe. Had an owl with a busted wing; said the danged fool had flown smack into the side of his wall."

He'd been polite, courteous, had had them in for coffee and store cookies. He'd even promised to buy some flares to use as distress signals.

"Cozy as a bug in a rug," had been their opinion.

A man who had cut himself off from his fellow men could have a mental quirk, the elder Lewin said. One didn't know to what lengths he'd go to protect his privacy.

Della, flipping pages, had written quite a list of things she wanted to buy before she came to the pages advertising furniture. There she was stopped by memories. This modern, clean-lined divan, for instance, was what she and Max had wanted. Their home, they had decided, was to be free from any sense of clutter; completely free of the many little gadgets Lottie had around.

But she wasn't thinking of Max. To put him out of her mind, she thought of Jack.

Max, too, was having a little difficulty remembering her. A classmate, hearing that Della had disappeared and also that she had broken their engagement, had briefed a young sister-in-law. Not, he told his wife, that he wanted to be rid of her, but Max was a catch. If Yvonne played her cards right, she'd be fixed for life.

Yvonne was doing her best. She'd spent the whole day grooming and dressing for the big event. But her mind, not too big at best, was so confused by the orders given by her sister and brother-in-law that she was rather overdoing it.

And she was wearing pink! To Max she symbolized another trap ready to be sprung; pretty as a picture, cute, but a trap.

Finally Della's mind slipped back to the forbidden subject of Earl Cross, conjecturing, wondering what Jack could posibly do about him, how he could learn his true condition.

By then Jack had tramped up the barely discernible path between the old corduroy road and the cabin of the man called Carl Elwood.

"Carl," he called, "it's Jack Lewin."

He heard a sound of things being pushed along the wood floor; then the door opened and the man stood in the doorway, stood in such a fashion that Jack was blocked from entering or even looking in.

8

"CARL," Jack drew a deep breath, "I need some help. May I come in and talk to you?"

"What kind of help?" the man asked suspiciously.

"We're sheltering a girl. She gave me the name of her doctor. I telephoned him from town; didn't give my name, and he didn't want it. The one law he laid down was that her privacy should be protected. She was to be given a chance to get her nerves under control before anyone got to her."

"Has anyone tried?" came the eager question.

"No. I think she was desperate enough to throw whoever it was completely off her trail. I think, from the time I met her at the café, she started out after dark. She was here shortly after sunrise. She also said the note she left would keep this person from trying."

"Where do I come into this? But first, why did she come here?"

He was backing into the cabin, offering a chair to Jack, though he still stood.

"Association of ideas," Jack told him, and recounted their conversation at a gas station some time before.

"Someone she loved had told her about Skyhigh, a mountain top lost in the clouds. She asked about the roads, and I warned her they weren't for Sunday drivers; told her this was a ghost town. I have a pretty good idea she'd tried to get away to other places; this was a last resort."

"Last resort." The man sank into an old rocker. "Now then, why did you come to me for help? Why not your father, a dozen others? Why me?"

"She was getting along pretty well until she saw you delivering the wood; then she had a relapse. I think she was afraid you'd get in touch with the person who's given her such a tough time."

"Me?" He was out of the chair. "I'd be the last, the very last. Jack, if that girl has run out, I'll put up a tent in the woods and stand guard twenty-four hours a day. Son, you don't know."

Jack looked around the room. There were no books; there were cartons. There were no dishes; again there were cartons.

"You thought she'd come here to spy on you?" he asked curiously.

"What else? When I saw that car camouflaged, I had to investigate. I saw the owner's name; the sister of a woman who never fought but never gave up. The ancient Chinese had the right idea of torture: that single drop of water. I wasn't going back to it."

"And now?"

The man Jack knew as Carl Elwood sat shaking his head. "I don't know. You have no conception of the sly lengths to which this woman would go to win her way."

"I think I have. This girl looked sick enough the first time I saw her. Ten days later I was almost afraid to have her on the place. That's why I called his city psychiatrist. He darned near backed off the phone to keep me from telling him who I was or her whereabouts.

"Dad and I worked it out this way. If he knew, he might come up here to check and inadvertently act as a decoy. The fact I'd called proved our concern for he girl. I told him Dad had been a patient of an associate of his, Geardon; that Dad had had the same condition, and that we'd call him if she needed him."

"She's that badly off?" He answered his own question. "She could be. Laura got out. Oh, I take the town paper; I keep up with things. This girl was all there was left. And I'm responsible. Now what do you want me to do?"

Jack's hands went out. "I don't know; what do you suggest? I don't even know the setup. Looks like both of you ran away from someone, but how do we know it's the same person?"

Carl asked Jack to think back, to try to remember anything the girl had said that might throw some light on the subject. Eventually Jack remembered one remark.

"She said she preferred bears and cougars to good people who manipulated affairs behind your back and wouldn't let you take a breath without supervision."

"That's the answer." In his excitement the man stood up. "All right; I'm ready to go back and face the music."

"Not yet," Jack argued. "This can wait until she is ready. Someone might be curious about your background and accidentally identify her."

The elder Lewin, slightly worried about Jack's long absence, decided to visit the cabin. "Thought you might have sprawled and broken a leg," he apologized.

"Just the fellow we want," both younger men said.

And Mrs. Lewin watched the windows and waited wondering what was keeping both of her men.

Della awakened to the soft thrumming of rain on the low roof. For a moment she lay relaxed. Today she would see Mr. Lewin about the purchase of this haven; then she would ask him to send off the order she'd drawn up the previous night.

Once this place was her own, no one could come onto the property without her permission. She could even, if she desired, have a high fence built on the land side; the sharp cliff to the west and south provided protection there.

Then came a sharp memory of Earl, and with it distress.

The Lewins waited for the thin spiral of smoke from the cabin chimney; the two men argued with Mrs. Lewin.

"Tell her everything," she insisted. "We women are greater realists than you."

When Jack came down he found the little place in order, Della looking better than he had ever seen her. That is, until she saw him; then anxious lines appeared.

Having been prompted by his mother, he prefaced his greeting with, "The news is all good. It is not amnesia. The poor fellow was packing, getting ready to run, because he'd checked your car and identified you."

"He thought I was after him?" cried Della.

"After I reassured him, he was ready to go back and face things. I warned him not to at this time. Someone checking on his immediate past might find you."

Della sank back into an old rocker. "He'd do that for me: go back?"

"He won't have any real peace of mind until he does. Temporary escape is like a military maneuver:

retreat to build up one's forces. But until a fellow conquers his enemy, he'll always be on the run."

She nodded her agreement. She was in retreat. She had come to this place to regain her health, and while she had no intention of ever living with Lottie again, she had every intention of returning eventually to establish her rights.

From Jack she learned Earl had told the Lewins everything and found relief in talking it out. He had planned his original escape for months, had worked out each detail. He'd chosen a time of the year when there would be no danger to woodsmen or cattle from the plane crash.

"He said he knew he was taking a hundred to one chance on coming out of it alive, but that one chance was worth it. He'd rather be dead than go on as he had been."

Della sat listening to the hiss of the rain at the windows, the crackle of the fire. She was aware Jack was watching her, worried at what he was telling her.

"It's so good to know this," she murmured; "it is confirmation of the fact that I've done right. You see, Jack, she is so good one feels like a monster ever going against her slightest wish.

"They seemed so devoted. Their marriage was something out of a story book."

He gave a short laugh. "How old were you when it took place?"

"Eleven."

"And your sister Laura?"

"Almost eighteen. But why do you mention her?"

"Earl, who was twenty then, had been secretly engaged to Laura; they were waiting for her eighteenth birthday to announce it. Then Laura fell for someone else and Lottie caught him on the rebound."

"Oh, no," cried Della. "That couldn't be. Laura

never cared about men at all. When she finally eloped
with Moulton we were shocked."

But now she was remembering Laura crying as if
her heart would break; then so defiant that Lottie
and her father had sent her to his parents' in Washington so she wouldn't ruin Lottie's wedding.

"They sent her away so fast they had to ship her
clothes," she murmured. And then, "I'll bet Lottie
planned that."

Just as she had conjured up the Viking at the
beach for Max to consider.

"But he didn't have to marry Lottie," she protested, "had he had any will of his own at all—"

"It wasn't will. He had reached the point a lot of
young fellows reach. When they lose their first love
they think the world has come to an end.

"He told me his mother was gravely ill; she preferred Lottie to Laura. Lottie lived up to the mother's
conception of her; Lottie cared for her until her
death."

"Four years later," agreed Della.

"He stood by five more years, hating every minute of it and hating himself because he couldn't appreciate what Lottie had done."

How well she knew that feeling.

He said he'd tried to make the best of a bad bar-
gain and had finally given up.

"Then why didn't he arrange things so she could
divorce him?" Della cried.

"In the first place, he knew she wouldn't. In the
second, as long as his death was still unconfirmed he
was saving some other poor devil from being
trapped."

"By her gentle goodness," agreed Della. "Nor
would she have given him a divorce under any cir-
cumstances." She added soberly, "Nor will she now."

After he had left, Della remembered his advice.

The problem of Lottie and Earl was not hers; she need not worry or even think about the outcome.

Yet how interrelated were their problems. Had Earl not run away, Lottie would not have come home, Laura made that unfortunate marriage, nor he be in hiding.

At noon, standing on the small porch looking into a fine web of rain, Della became aware of something that lifted her spirits. She had gone through an entire morning without a tremor of nerves; a difficult morning at that. She would win out.

Given enough time, she would regain her health and go back to face Lottie and Max.

Della went in to look through the books Lewin had brought down; she was ready now to look through case histories of others like herself, to learn how they had conquered their fears.

Mrs. Lewin stood at the dining room door. First Jack, then her husband had walked blithely in, and on the shining floor she had just waxed were gobs of mud, black and brown islands in a sea of perfection.

"I swear to goodness," her voice rose and her waxer smashed down, "any woman with two men in her house should have her head examined. Of all the thoughtless, careless creatures in the world—"

"Well, if you think for one minute I'm going to stand outside my own home and ask permission to enter—"

"Yeah," Jack followed his father's lead. "Why don't you wait to wax until we're away?"

Startled, Mrs. Lewin looked at them. Neither seemed the least abashed or guilty. Solemnly first one, then the other, came over to kiss her.

"Now had you been a really good woman," Mr. Lewin intoned soberly, "you wouldn't have let off steam. You'd have demonstrated gentle resignation for hours and let us stew, wondering what we'd done this time."

"And locked us out for hours the next time you waxed. When do we eat?"

"After you've cleaned up the mess you've made," said Mrs. Lewin airily, her exasperation gone. "I might even let you cut into the huckleberry pie this noon. Our last jar of berries until they ripen again, so appreciate them."

Della had a piece of the pie that evening. Jack had said she wanted to talk to his mother, and gladly Mrs. Lewin had trotted down, raincoat over her head.

"Isn't this weather awful?" she greeted Della. "I love it. Gives me an excuse to scold my men."

Della looked at the shining face. "I'll bet they enjoy it as much as you do."

"Could be. Now then, shall we talk about the grocery order? We try to drive in to the nearest big town once a week for general supplies. What would you like us to bring you?"

Della admitted she didn't know, that she needed advice. Such cooking as she had done had been during summer vacations when her sister Laura and her father were working and everyone was hungry.

"Tell you what. You buy what appeals to you, cook it, then poke what you don't want in our deep freeze. We've plenty of room this time of year. No need growing tired of a thing before you're through with it."

Here was another test. Memory winged back to the hours she'd spent poring over cook books for two, always with the dream of Max across a small table.

Mrs. Lewin watched the hands tense, saw the jaw line grow rigid and, because she had lived with it, understood.

"Why not let me browse, take advantage of sales?

I had a taste of cooking for myself when Jack was in the service and Dad up here."

"But I must overcome this," Della replied through set teeth.

"Not now. Easy does it. If you trust me, why not get this off your chest? There is man talk and there is woman talk. We're women."

A very sober mother walked back through the rain. She'd left a crying girl behind her. Tears were good, cleansing the spirit. Dr. Geardon had told John a good percentage of tensions were built up in children who were taught it was wrong to cry. Nature provided tears as vents, release from grief or frustration.

Fortunately, neither of her men folk noticed her absorption. Jack had come in and automatically switched on the radio to catch the five o'clock news.

The first story held them spellbound.

"A prominent valley woman involved in a two-car accident this afternoon has sent out a call to her sister, Della Donovan, now motoring some place in the state. Mrs. Charlotte Cross, of Valley City, has suffered injuries, the extent of which are not yet determined, and is asking police and citizens to contact her younger sister if possible. The car license number is—"

Both men jumped up and looked down the hill to where the car stood well hidden by fir boughs.

"She will be remembered as the widow of the late Earl Cross, who disappeared four years ago in a light plane over the Siskivous. Wreckage of the plane was later found in a remote area, but—"

Jack's hands went up. "Now what do we do? Do we dare keep still?"

9

Lewin senior spoke first. "If she were dying the announcer would have said so. Let's wait for the six o'clock television news. They'll probably have pictures of the wreck."

"Why can't you call Dr. Geardon and have him check?" asked his wife. "If you ask me, I'd say this woman had that accident on purpose. Now don't look so skeptical; women have been known to attempt suicide to bring men to heel. From what I heard today, this Lottie would stop at nothing."

"Della," Jack sprang up, "brought her transistor with her."

"Oh, sit down," snapped his mother. "She's not listening to news on purpose. She said so. I invited her up to watch TV, and she said she couldn't yet; even the tension in a comedy got her on edge. As for music, she feels most of it is being played on her nerves."

"And Earl?"

He answered for them. He came pounding up to the doorway. "Don't you let Della go to her," he stormed. "She broke an ankle to keep me from going into a lookout our first summer. She enjoys it."

The four sat close to the television set.

"You folks listen; I'll watch," Earl ordered.

There were pictures of the two cars and one of a bewildered man, the driver of a for-hire car, who said Mrs. Cross had insisted upon sitting with him and had grabbed the wheel at the wrong moment, forcing the sideswipe which had sent his vehicle into a wooded ditch.

And there was one very sharp picture of Mrs. Lottie Cross as the guerney was being lifted into an ambulance.

"Ha," intoned Cross, "I've seen that look a hundred times."

"Sh," warned the others.

"Latest reports from Sacred Heart Hospital indicate the injuries sustained by Mrs. Cross are painful but not serious; however, she will be confined to her bed for an indeterminate period of time. For this reason police and private citizens have been requested to contact her vacationing sister Della Donovan, now motoring through the state."

Cross shook his head. "Of all the Machiavellian schemes. Everybody and his dog will be watching for Della's car from now until the heat wears off."

Ninety miles southeast, Max Mayer, sitting down before his television for a pre-dinner session with his pipe, straightened. Someone would get in touch with Della. She would return. And then—

"That blasted pink apartment. I won't do it. Della ran out on me," he said aloud.

Angrily he jumped up and threw his tasteless pipe aside; the bowl, which had been the pride of his college days, cracked. In another moment he was at the telephone, calling the sister-in-law of his friend.

"One thing about her," he said defensively, "she chatters so much I can't think."

The telephone rang before he got away. Reluctantly he answered.

"Max," came a feminine voice, "this is Ruth. Don't you dare give Della's address to Lottie. She'll stop at nothing to get her back. She's even combing California. Laura wrote me she'd had private detectives in her hair for days."

"Laura? You mean the no-good sister?"

"Listen, you halfwit, the only difference between Laura and Della is this: Della had sense enough to escape *before* marriage."

Mayer's ears tingled with the bang of her receiver.

Nor was Dr. Dan too happy. Innocently he accepted a call from Sacred Heart Hospital right in the middle of his well earned dinner. He was even professionally sympathetic when told a patient involved in a motor accident was calling for him. He froze and used words not found in medical books when the patient's name was finally revealed.

"Call you back," he barked.

"Dan," reproved his wife a few moments later, "for a man who claims to be an authority upon the meanderings of the mind—"

"That darned woman!" he slapped down his napkin. "I'm going to have to see her to shut her up. Not that I'll be able to help my patient through her. And darn ethics," he added. "I'd like to put her into hypnosis and load her with post-hypnotic suggestions that would make a decent woman of her."

"You mean she isn't—"

"She is good," he said gravely; "she is so confounded good she can't be fought. Good on the surface, that is." He spoke dreamily. "It would be quite a treat to get down under that surface of hers. Educational."

"Dear, did you watch the news? There was the strangest accident. A woman, painfully injured, sent out a call to a sister motoring some place in the state."

"Della Donovan?" he barked.

"Why, dear, you did—"

"Great Scott!" said Dr. Dan, and jumped up so fast his coffee cup didn't try to follow, but did leave a brown stain on white linen.

"Geardon," he literally shouted a few moments later, "get hold of that ex-patient of yours and have him barricade the doors."

In another moment he admitted he didn't know the extent of the woman's injuries. Geardon was to call the hospital, find out and then call the ex-patient.

Everyone in the Lewin household jumped when the telephone rang. Lewin senior was nearest.

"Well," he beamed on the family as he returned, "our girl's doctor has a prime idea where she's hiding out. Geardon just called to discuss a motor accident. He had been in conference with the attending physician and was happy to report the woman involved, Mrs. Lottie or Earl Cross, had contusions, abrasions, purported shock and would be lying on her face for a few days. Aside from that she is in excellent condition. No need for anyone to feel any concern whatsoever."

A sibilant sigh went up from his audience; then Jack spoke in a shocked voice. "Dad, suppose she hadn't come here to us. Anyone else would have run to the nearest telephone. She'd have been plunged back with her old life before she was ready."

"Well, son," Mrs. Lewin soothed him, "I think the good Lord has a way of looking after the Dellas of the world, if they give Him a chance."

Della pulled raincoat and hood over her head the next morning and started uphill. She'd been on the place just over a week, and this was the first time she'd dared leave the cabin. Oh, she was improving. The thought gave a spring to her step.

Jack had already left on a log-haul, but his father saw her approach and blurted, "I hope to high heaven she hasn't used her radio."

"We'll tell her," decided Mrs. Lewin. "You trot along; I'll handle this."

"Now, Mother—"

"Oh, stop acting like an anxious hen and get out."

Lewin was still laughing when he greeted Della, and when she entered the kitchen Mrs. Lewin was, too. "Men," she explained. "Father was in a tizzy because I insisted upon giving you some good news about your sister Lottie."

"Good news?" stammered Della.

"I'll say. She won't be able to sit down for a week. Dad called his doctor in the city and asked him to check on a 'friend,' to find out her true condition. He knew Geardon wouldn't repeat the news of the call; asked him not to, in fact."

"But what happened?"

"If you ask me," Mrs. Lewin replied, "I'd say she tried to frame a minor accident, probably as an inducement to get you home to nurse her. But it backfired. She grabbed the wheel of a for-hire car at the right moment; the car sideswiped another, the door on her side flew open and she sat down, way down, in a ditch.

"She was," Mrs. Lewin looked like an owl, "all shook up."

"Oh, poor Lottie. She may be—"

"Ah-ah," warned Mrs. Lewin. "This brother-in-law of yours tells us she broke an ankle to keep him from going on with his forestry work. He said she had a wonderful time. Proved to him he couldn't be away for extended periods. Before he knew what had happened, he was set up in a general merchandise store."

Mrs. Lewin reached for the bottle of pills which had come through the mails, a repeat of a prescription Mr. Lewin had once used. A mild sedative was indicated at the moment.

"It's so difficult to learn to hate her," Della apologized.

"My goodness, child, you don't have to hate her or anyone else. That's no solution."

"But—" Della held her coffee cup for a second helping.

"Here, try this coffee cake. Dad had a co-worker in the city he let wreck him. One day I looked out a window and nearly called the man in the white jacket. Father was swinging one long leg in a most peculiar fashion.

"'I'm hinged wrong,' he said when I burst out. 'Just trying to kick myself for letting that so-and-so get close enough to me to harm me.'"

Della digested the wisdom and the coffee cake, then told why she had come up to the house, and Mrs. Lewin approved. "Nothing like a bit of garden to get the kinks out of soul and body."

Before starting home, Della turned back and asked the questions Mrs. Lewin had been afraid she'd ask.

"Yes, Della, she did send out a radio and television plea for your return. She said you were on vacation, motoring around the state. That's why Father had to learn the extent of her injuries. Now, don't get jittery. Nobody here will ever report you. Earl is coming to do some hoeing for us today while we're away."

"You needn't see him. Actually, he needn't be here. It was his idea. You see, child, he hasn't been cured of his hatred, so fear still rides his life."

Della raced down the hill to draw the walls of the grey cabin about her.

At that moment Dr. Dan was standing outside the private room occupied by Mrs. Charlotte Cross. He had studied her chart; now he'd been detained by her physician.

"As far as her physical condition is concerned," said the latter, "I should be sending her home to release the room for someone who needs it. However, she is in great mental distress. She's reliving the period of time after her husband's disappearance and is convinced her sister has met with an accident. If there is anything you can do—"

"What she needs," stated Dr. Dan bluntly, "is mental surgery, but the condition is so chronic I doubt she would survive."

"I understand." Gravely the other nodded. "She is so gentle any deep probing could—"

"My dear Fergie," snapped Dr. Dan, "that woman has the mind of an old range cow; as tough and as stubborn. She knows all the trails, and she's not about to let herself be led to new pastures. I'll see her."

He did. Lottie tried to win him over. She called attention to her physical condition and wasn't consoled to hear him say she herself was responsible and knew it.

"I'm sorry you've been so prejudiced against me," she said forgivingly, "but you do see how necessary it is for me to have Della at home during my convalesence."

"Again you can blame yourself," he stated relentlessly. "Had you allowed her the privacy I ordered for her, you would have known how to reach her. I'm quite sure you can afford a practical nurse in your home, or do you prefer a girl who is ill to wait on you?"

She tried tears, but they weren't very effective.

After all, she was lying on her face, more or less. There was quite a bit about the ingratitude of those she had helped. Even Della's fiancé had turned against her, and she'd planned a glorious future for him.

Pitifully she cried, "Why, oh why, is everyone I love taken from me?"

Dr. Dan looked at his watch. "If you are sincere about wanting to know, come to me professionally. Until you have a desire for the truth, I can do nothing for you."

His office attendant and nurses all reported a handsome young man had been around while he was making hospital calls. With each the young man brought up the subject of the accident the day before.

"Did you tell him anything?"

"No, but we ate his chocolates."

Dr. Dan called Geardon to meet him at the club for lunch; at that stage he wasn't trusting even the telephone.

"Our fishing trip's off," he announced. "I'm being tailed."

"Well, good. I have a better idea; let's take the tailers off on a wild goose chase. How's your wind these days? I know a wicked place to reach, straight up. No fish, but a whale of a good spot to sleep."

Lottie's detectives, faithfully trailing, lost much of their enthusiasm for their job that weekend.

"And us without even a pup tent," mourned one to the director of the agency.

"Honest, all those two guys did was sleep," reported the other. "Didn't make a single contact any place. Didn't do a doggone thing but sleep and cook over a pint-size stove. Smelled good."

"Lucky guys," said the director wistfully.

"Any new leads?"

There had been calls from all over the state, from

Washington, Idaho, northern California and one from Nevada. The number of persons who had seen Della Donovan was astonishing—only it was never Della.

"Probably living right here in town; had the car painted. Larry, you check the quick car paint spots. Jim, look up that friend of yours again. If she sells her car, we'll at least have a starting point.

"You know, if this Cross woman wan't such a nice, gentle sort of woman—"

"And wasn't such good pay?"

"—I'd call it off. Well, maybe the sister will have the common decency to let her know she's all right, at least."

Nothing was further from the sister's mind. She had been digging in damp soil. The soil was soft, but so were her muscles, and when she straightened she became aware of some she'd never known she possessed.

Life was good. She'd gone through this last crisis without a relapse. For two days now she'd had neither a tremor, nausea nor fit of panicky depression.

The day before she had cornered Mr. Lewin and paid one thousand dollars for this precious three-room cabin and four acres of ground. Imagine all of that for a thousand. Imagine having this magnificent view included in the purchase.

There had been only one hitch in the transaction. Della couldn't accept title to her purchase without revealing her location. After the extremes to which Lottie had gone, they could not be sure she wasn't having all property transfers checked.

Mr. Lewin had an attorney and a banker he could trust, so papers were drawn up, the money deposited, everything made ready to go into escrow when Della felt ready to face her sister.

Now Mrs. Lewin watched her son, in from his last

log haul, stand before a window a moment, then wheel in another direction. His mother went to the window and looked down.

"Oh, dear," she whimpered, "Jack—"

"He's only going to shave," Mr. Lewin reproved her.

"At this hour of the day? Father, you know what that means."

He mumbled he'd been young once, but she didn't hear. That girl down there had been deeply in love with one man for years. Could she escape love? And if not, where did her loyalty lie?

10

DELLA turned to look at the cabin, saw a figure there, and her heart lurched. Then she recognized Jack in fresh sun-tans and hurried toward him.

He met her halfway. "Della you don't look like the same girl. You look wonderful, with color in your cheeks, your eyes sparkling. I'd say you could go out and conquer the world."

"Thank you, kind sir," she gave a mocking bow, "but would you mind if I waited until I have my subconscious trained to realize it? Your father sent down a wonderful book on changing habits. I'm making progress, I think, but my habit is very stubborn and very ingrained."

Jack led her back to the little porch where he'd left a frosted pitcher of fruit juice sent down by his mother.

Love, he reasoned, could be a habit. Earl had told him about Max, something he hadn't divulged to his mother. Earl had told him Della had had many boy friends during school and college days but only one for whom she really cared.

He had pulled out newspapers from a drawer to show him stories and photographs of the announcement party, the approaching marriage, even the date.

Earl had angrily underscored one line: "The young couple plan to move to an apartment in the Donovan home."

Earl didn't know what had happened. Except for that line, he would have said Lottie had broken up the affair.

Della came out from washing garden grime from her hands, and Jack looked at her ring finger. She had worn a ring, he could tell, but it was no longer there.

The last weekly had carried a brief note on the postponement of the wedding for "a month." Yet he knew Della had no intention of returning.

Was love a habit and could it be broken? That was his problem.

"Della," he began, "the subconscious isn't stubborn. If it were, habits couldn't be formed so easily. It's only too willing to carry out orders. But it's so automatic it goes merrily on with its old thought patterns until those are firmly changed. The best method is to reverse them."

"I don't think I understand," she said, settling comfortably into the old wooden rocker.

"How are you handling the nerve condition you had when you came up? How did you feel before you went to Dr. Dan, and what have you done to change?"

"Oh, that."

For a moment grey depression hovered as she thought of the last weeks at her home.

"First I got away from the cause," she began thoughtfully, "as Dr. Dan said, to regain my strength. The sedation he gave me eased the attacks so they weren't so dreadful, and naturally my fear was less. And then—"

She thought of the unpacking she had had to do.

"I told myself I didn't have to have attacks any more because the cause wasn't there. That's it." She turned a shining face to Jack. "That's what I've been doing: talking to myself like a Dutch uncle. Sometimes I'd say, 'Oh, cut it out; that's over.' Sometimes I'd say, 'Don't be a dope; why suffer when you don't have to?' "

"And what would happen?"

She laughed. "It's silly, but I can't remember. I think I'd be so busy doing something I'd forget about an attack starting and wouldn't know when it quit."

"In other words, you were giving orders, reversing previous orders. And it worked."

Della felt as though he had handed her a priceless gift. He had made her aware she was in control of her own life. Now she could think of Lottie and even of Max without fear of that silly sickness.

"My goodness," she breathed, "Lottie started training me twenty years ago. From the time I was a toddler her word was law. Even when she wasn't living with us it never occurred to me I didn't have to obey.

"Yet here in this short time I've learned that I needn't. Jack, my subconscious is a grand little guy. Now that I know how to handle him, we're going to get along."

He added a final word before they went out to check fresh plots he would spade for her.

"That rule can work in a lot of ways, Della. You don't have to be burdened with any old thought habits or emotional entanglements."

When Jack reached home his mother had come to a grim decision. No girl, not even one she loved as she did Della, was going to ruin the life of her only son.

"Son, there is something I have to tell you. Della confided in me. Jack, Della has a young man."

"Max Maver?" he asked. "Yes, I know all about him. Earl showed me clippings from the home town newspaper."

"Well, what have you been doing?" she asked, deflated.

"Spade work." He grinned at her, chucked her under the chin and said, "When do we eat?"

"Men!" his mother spat at him.

Charlotte was carried back to Valley City without much chance to view the world about her. She didn't mind: she was viewing the world within.

Friends and neighbors were gathered to watch her return, and she made the most of it. She could hear them say, "Poor Lottie; a martyr to her family. Wouldn't you think that girl would come home and look after her?"

Dr. Ken had hired the nurse. Dr. Ken liked nurses, respected them and, as he told his wife, was doggoned if he was going to sacrifice one to Lottie's gentle whims.

So he had installed one affectionately known as "old horse face." Perversely, she had the disposition of a mule. She wasn't to be ridden.

"Out," said this Mrs. Harrigan as friends and neighbors started filing in, hoping for tidbits of news. "Our patient has had a trying trip. Out."

They departed. Lottie protested. She wept a little. Mrs. Harrigan merely turned her face up so she could dry her tears without soiling the linen.

Another change in Lottie's plans had been made. She was not in the downstairs bedroom but had been carried up to her own. This, she knew, gave this hard-faced nurse a chance to screen callers, to keep them out without Lottie knowing it.

"She'll heal quicker upstairs," Dr. Ken told Mrs. Harrigan. "Leave her down where she'll be surrounded by admirers and she'll be good for two months at least. We'll establish hospital visiting hours and hold the visitors to one at a time. That will cure her, fast."

Lottie decided to discharge the nurse, but Dr. Ken warned her no others were available and no neighbor or friend was going to remain with her indefinitely. They all had lives of their own.

She decided to discharge Dr. Ken because he no longer had her interests at heart. He said, "By all means do so, but remember I owe it to my reputation to give those you tell a true explanation." And she, wondering what that might be, changed her mind.

She had Nurse Harrigan send for Max, but Max, she learned, was busy.

"Busy with that Yvonne something or other; you know, Ted Neilsen's sister-in-law," said a caller.

"Hm," said Lottie, and thought of the pink apartment. Well, once Della was over her pettishness and home, she'd find a much better husband for her. Meanwhile she would think of Max.

She did, for hours. When her next caller came in, she started her campaign. Della had changed when Max Mayer came into her life. Actually Della had run away because she had found him out and couldn't bring herself to marry him. Poor darling little sister.

"I'd tried so hard to like him, she believed I did and couldn't come to me in her hour of distress."

"Lottie is such a good woman she defeats her own ends," the caller concluded, after passing on the news.

The story had grown considerably by the time it

eached Max. Irate, he went to a senior partner, determined to sue the woman for defamation of character.

"You couldn't win," he was told. "Put that good woman on the stand, and the jury would weep with her. Just thank your lucky stars Della took a run-out powder. And while you're about it, consider what her life has been and what courage it took for her to give you up in order to be rid of her sister as well."

"That," blurted Max, "was my own bone-headed fault. I fell for Lottie's goodness and worked with her. Della found out and left both of us."

"The poor kid," mused the older man. "She had her whole world cut out from under her at one fell swoop. Hope she's all right. No word of her, I suppose?"

Max almost reconsidered Lottie's invitation to call. He blamed himself for not seeing Della's problem from her viewpoint. And for the first time he forgot himself completely and began worrying about her.

He called on Ruth that evening and let her know of his change of heart, but she was of no help in locating Della.

"And I'd like to. Laura keeps writing demanding I find Della so she can look after her."

"If you ask me, she's had too much looking after by her sisters. But, Ruth, think back. Didn't she ever mention a place she might like to visit? Haven't you any clue at all?"

Ruth had one, but it was so ridiculous she didn't give it credence, nor did she know how to follow it up. On that drive back from the city, she had asked what Della and the log trucker had talked about. Now what had Della said? Oh yes, he came from some place Lottie's husband had liked, a place Earl Cross had said was "lost in the clouds."

"You've thought of something," Max charged.

"Sort of, but I don't know how to follow it up and still keep my husband."

"Tell me and I'll do it."

"Oh, no. Not that I don't trust you, Max, but how do we know Lottie isn't having us watched? Besides, you might get curious."

"All I want to know is how she's feeling; that she's all right."

"We'd have heard if she wasn't."

Ruth talked it over with her husband that night. He said he would try on his next trip to the city. He could ask questions she couldn't ask.

He wasn't too happy when she gave the description of the man. "The handsomest I've ever seen: tall, broad shoulders, slim hips. Dark hair that waves back like I'd like mine to wave, beautiful dark eyes and teeth that belong in a dental ad. And when he smiles, oh my!"

"I'll go tomorrow. Need a change of oil and a lube job; that will give me a chance to stick around and ask questions."

Ruth told him the approximate time they'd reached the station, and Don Brewer arrived shortly before.

He'd been there half an hour when an empty log truck pulled up, driven by a man who answered Ruth's description. Don sized him up and decided truth was going to work best with this fellow.

"I'm Don Brewer," he said, extending his hand, "and I've been delegated to ask you some questions. My wife," he added with a wry smile, "was the delegator."

"About what?" snapped Jack.

"Around six weeks ago my wife took a friend to a Dr. Dan Kendall in the city. My wife's name is Ruth; she's so high, with brown hair, and a little on the plump side. She was wearing a grey suit that day and one of those darned fool hats that look like beehives."

Jack's memory flashed back. He'd noticed the hat on Della's friend, and now he was wary.

"A short time after this, the friend disappeared, vanished into thin air. She wrote Ruth not to worry and also asked her to send a message to a sister, Laura, if Ruth could learn her whereabouts. She did. Since then Ruth's been bombarded by telegrams, phone calls and letters from Laura, who wants to find this girl, Della. Then yesterday Della's ex-fiancé came over to harry her. She didn't let on to him he'd struck a memory chord; instead she appointed me."

"Look, fellow, this is all very interesting, but where do I come in?"

Don looked around; this wasn't the place to go into things. "Don't you take a coffee break or something? Let's finish this in the café."

Jack agreed.

In the café, in a booth, Don took up the story. Della had felt faint. Some trucker had walked her back to the Brewer car and somehow, somewhere along the line, had referred to a place Earl Cross had loved, a place "lost in the clouds."

"Della had exhausted every other known place as a hideout, so my wife thought maybe she'd gone there."

Jack said yes; now he remembered the girl. He'd thought she was going to pass out on him. He also said, "It seems to me your wife and this ex-fiancé of hers should let her alone if they have her interests at heart. She sure looked shot that day."

And then he had a harrowing thought. All this Brewer would have to do would be to take the

license number of his truck, check with the state
motor vehicle department and learn his home address. Then he and this Max, and perhaps the sister
as well, could drive up to Skyhigh.

11

DON BREWER knew the moment Jack had this thought. He took time out to marvel at the intuitive faculties of women, his wife in particular, then spoke.

"There's something I'd like to get over to you. Neither my wife nor this ex-fiancé want to find her. Above all, they don't want her back where she was. It was Ruth who framed her to get her to the psychiatrist. If anyone doesn't believe that, they can check with Doctor Dan.

"All the wife and Max—he's the ex-fiancé—"

"What ex?"

"Oh, he fell for the sister's line. He knew the girl had changed terrifically and backed the older woman when she planned to put her in a rest home; even worked with her. Della, whom this Lottie thought she had put out with a sleeping pill, overheard. That did it."

"How does he feel now?"

"I wouldn't know, but a fellow at the club said he acted as if a load had been lifted. He wasn't keen on moving into the old Donovan house after their marriage. As I started to say, all these two want is to know she's all right. Ruth feels responsible because she took her to the psychiatrist, and she would like to get Laura's letters to her. Okay, fellow, now how about it?"

Jack chose his words carefully. "I'm not going to tell you the place I mentioned that day because I don't feel it's my right. I will do this. I'll go there this weekend and scout around. If you want to leave the letters here at the station in my name, I'll pick them up and, if I find her, deliver them.

"I'll also drop you a line if I find her and she okays it."

"I'll give you the letters now; if you don't locate Della, you can leave them here in my name. I'll be back a week from today."

Jack drove home in a thoughtful mood. It seemed strange a girl couldn't escape without leaving some trace. How was Della going to take this? Above all, just how in the deuce was he going to tell her without causing another emotional upset?

Why couldn't people leave her alone?

Well, he had until the weekend to think it over.

Jack rolled his truck onto a graveled patch inside the big yard and started for the house. There was the former fiancé. Could be the guy meant he wanted her to have time to get well, that he knew she needed to be alone.

"On the other hand," he said aloud, "why did he let her get into—"

Della was standing before him, curls wind-blown, her first tan touched with crimson. "My-my." she chided. "when a man talks to himself and about a girl—Blonde?"

"Brother, I wish she were."

"So you're a　gentlemen? Well, your mother

says, 'Tell Jackie to wash up and come out to the summerhouse before the food dries out.' Hurry."

He hurried half-heartedly. What should have been a time of rejoicing at Della's joining the family group would be marred if he didn't watch himself.

Della was enjoying everything.

"I could tackle wildcats," she said, happily.

"I could even ask," she continued, "how you happen to have a letter from my sister Laura in your shirt pocket."

Jack nearly upset the table.

"Nope, not second sight; just that familiar things catch one's eye. How could you find her address when I couldn't?"

Jack floundered until his father came to the rescue. "Truth is better in the long run," he commented.

"Your friend Ruth remembered our meeting," he blurted. "Her husband was there today to give me these."

"Jack, you didn't tell him?" began Mrs. Lewin.

"Didn't have to. He asked me to recall a meeting with a girl about to faint; the name of the place I'd mentioned which had had such an impact. Two cups of coffee later I made a choice between having him run down my license number and show up here, or evading the issue.

"I told him I remembered, that I'd scout that area this weekend, and, if Della was there, would deliver the letters."

"And report back?"

"Only that she was all right. I worked that angle coming up. I'll mail a letter to the gas station to be held for him; then I'll choose another stop miles from there."

"Ruth's all right," Della said easily.

"But Ruth," he informed her, "isn't sure she isn't being watched."

The sun slid behind the horizon and a chill fell on the summerhouse. Della wanted to say, "I'm up to fighting wildcats but not Lottie. There's no place to grab a hold."

Dinner over, Mrs. Lewin insisted Della run along home. The Lewins had their cook-outs down to a science. They would have to revamp their routine if they had help.

Jack walked with her, troubled by his part in exposing her general whereabouts.

"He really had me over a barrel," he confessed, "though at no time did he ask if I'd ever seen you again. What I can't understand is how he identified me as the man you'd talked to."

A thoroughly feminine giggle came from Della, startling him and herself as well. How long since she had laughed like that?

"Ruth was quite struck by your looks, Jack. When she mentioned it, I tried to look back but couldn't see you."

"Well, that's something for my morale. You talked to me five or ten minutes and didn't see me; right?"

She nodded. "All of which makes me realize how dreadfully ill I was and how much I've improved."

He had to read into that what he could. By the time he was back at the summerhouse he felt quite cheerful about it.

"How does Della feel about the letters?" Mrs. Lewin asked.

"Good, as far as I know. I imagine she won't know until she reads them."

Della didn't know. She settled into a deep chair, a lamp at her shoulders, and sat holding the little packet. She wanted to bring Laura back into focus. They hadn't been too close. Seven years in childhood made a much greater difference than it would now.

Laura had been the antithesis of Lottie—outspoken, quick and fiery. One always knew exactly what she expected a person to do.

And scrappy, always fighting, Della thought. But that could have been Lottie's fault. Lottie could have antagonized her.

Slowly and at times painfully, Della read her way through the letters.

There was the first eager plea for Della to come south. She, Laura, had a fine position in an electronics plant; a two-bedroom cottage apartment. If she hadn't been able to pick up her money, Della should wire and she, Laura, would wire travel money to any name and address she suggested.

Later, after Laura had long-distanced Ruth, the letters contained affectionate complaints. Della should have left word with one person, someone like Ruth whom she could trust. No one better than she herself could know what an effect Lottie had on a person. Della wasn't fit to take care of herself after such a length of time under Lottie's velvet thumb.

"We have some of the best physicians and psychiatrists in the country around the University," Laura wrote. "Once you're here we'll have you straightened out in no time. Now call me the minute you receive this. If necessary I can come after you. You simply must have someone to look after you."

Mr. Lewin went out to watch the twilight. Somehow the view was better along the ledge.

Della saw his silhouette against the afterglow. Impulsively she sought his company. "Why can't they leave me alone?" she asked. "I want to think Laura is motivated by love for me, but somehow I can't. It's too much as though my going to her after running away from Lottie would prove to the world she, Laura, had been right."

"And it wouldn't?"

"If you know you're right, you don't need anyone else to prove it."

"Good girl. But let's look at it this way. She's worried about you; so is this friend Ruth and your friend Max!"

"Max!" Della stood tensed, ready to run.

"Now wait. Neither Ruth nor Max want you to return, nor do they want to see you, at least until you are ready. Both feel responsible for your escape from Lottie.

"This Brewer who talked to Jack said they feared you might fall into the wrong hands. If you could write Ruth and perhaps Laura, we'd have the letter mailed from a place they couldn't trace."

Della turned. "I'll do that."

"Wait. Not tonight. You have something to work out. Each crisis you have to face can be a blessing in disguise. Take the appearance of your brother-in-law. Didn't that help you? When you can, go back and evaluate. You'll be stronger, safer in the future. Now skip along; read that last book I handed you."

Della couldn't skip; by now it was too dark. She walked slowly, aware of the topaz lights in the cottage, *her* cottage which couldn't be taken from her by anyone.

Curiously she picked up the book Lewin senior had left when he'd been down to invite her to the cook-out. She'd expected philosophy, religion, even one of the old British mysteries, but this was a light, popular novel.

How could she read this or anything else with her first indirect message from Max in mind?

"Max feels responsible," she repeated, and a vision of Max sharp and clear flashed on her vision.

"He should!" she cried angrily. "If he hadn't let Lottie win him over—"

She stopped. She wouldn't have escaped. She wouldn't have come to this blessed little cabin where she was safe from intrusion. Her illness could have gone on and on until who knew what would have happened eventually?

"That still doesn't excuse him," she stated firmly, and prepared for bed.

She'd try to read the book. Thus far Mr. Lewin had been right. She'd accused him of providing escape avenues, and he had laughed and corrected her. "Retreat," he'd said; "time to rest your eyes and your mind so you can focus on the right perspective when necessary."

She read a few pages without a word getting through to her. Max felt responsible. She sat up. Why, that meant he'd finally seen through Lottie's maneuvering.

Doggedly she turned to the book reading aloud until finally it took over. Such a silly book; it poked fun at people with serious problems. Yet she couldn't help laughing a little. People took themselves so seriously.

On the verge of sleep, she had a mental picture of herself slipping out of the Donovan house, slippers in hand, of all of the ridiculous maneuvering she had done in those early hours to keep from leaving any trace, and it struck her funny.

"How silly can you get?" she whispered.

She awakened laughing at herself.

Of all the weak-kneed idiots, she reflected as she prepared breakfast. All any of us would have had to do was stand up to Lottie, pin her ears back at intervals.

While the coffee perked she raced out to water

some young plants, slipped and landed on her face in the mud.

Jack, just starting down with the milk, shouted for his father, and together they raced down to stand her up and wipe her off and find she was laughing, not crying.

"How on earth have you two put up with me?" she demanded. "I think I'm the funniest thing that ever happened to me."

Mrs. Lewin waited for the two men anxiously. "It's all right, Mother," they said in unison.

"Now the healing has really begun," Mr. Lewin observed. "She can laugh at herself."

Della borrowed Mr. Lewin's typewriter that day to write a riotous account of her adventures to Ruth and Laura. Ruth she blessed for kidnapping her and taking her to Dr. Dan, getting her on the right path, showing her how to unscramble her scrambled thinking.

To Laura she wrote more of her findings. "Like those three puppies we had, remember? One snapped, one cowered, and one just sat and did nothing. We should have joined forces like Rip and Cowie did and chewed the daylights out of Goodboy. We'd have made a man of Lottie and saved ourselves both a lot of heartaches."

She said she was still keeping her whereabouts a dark secret because she didn't know but what Lottie was having all of her friends watched. She was having such a wonderful time she didn't want to be found just yet. She had a love of a cottage, a garden, an older couple who were keeping an eye on her. She was resting, reading, eating and gaining weight.

To Ruth's letter she added a postscript: "If you see Max, thank him for joining forces with Lottie. It took that to jar me out of an impossible situation.

Had we gone on as we were, we'd have hated each other as well as ourselves."

Two days later an excited Ruth telephoned Max. "She's back," she cried.

"Della? Back at Lottie's?" he exclaimed incredulously.

"No, I mean the girl I knew in college is back. I've just had a letter from her. She's gay and happy like she used to be. And she's all right. Oh, and she sent a message to you."

Max was a very inattentive fourth at a dinner given that night to meet a visiting cousin of a friend. This one didn't talk with her lips; she used her eyebrows and rolled her eyes. He wondered how the dickens he was going to get out of seeing her again without hurting his friends. This was getting to be quite a problem. Take Yvonne. He wished heartily someone would.

Laura received her letter the following day, skimmed it and cried, "Well, of all the ingratitude!" Later she read it again and began building up defenses. She would never forgive Lottie for what she had done to Earl.

By chance she looked at a calendar. Della had run away a month ago. She hoped she'd been better prepared financially than she'd been. She, Laura, had known hunger. She'd learned at one time how to curl up in a haymow.

"Leave it to Lottie to see she didn't have any cash. The little dope, why didn't she send me an address so I could help her? I wonder how she's fixed for money."

Della wasn't wondering. She knew. She'd come down out of the clouds in which Skyhigh was supposed to be lost to rock bottom.

Here she'd been blithely resting on the assurance that, with the cabin paid for, she could live comfortably on her annuity of a hundred and fifty a month. She'd been so busy with her physical ailments she hadn't gotten around to realizing she couldn't collect that annuity without revealing her address.

Just how could even the most capable private secretary make a living in a ghost town?

"I'll starve to death before I'll leave," she cried.

12

Mrs. John Lewin was worried. When she was worried she talked to herself. Sometimes she answered herself back, aloud.

Husband and son, aware of this, would sit silent, hardly breathing, hoping their immobility might bring forth some gem of knowledge.

"No pot roast can last two weeks," stated Mrs. Lewin.

They waited.

"One loaf of bread in two weeks."

They exchanged puzzled glances.

"Margarine instead of butter, and no coffee at all."

Mrs. Lewin, they decided, must be considering a diet. Inwardly they shuddered. They'd been through this before when wife and mother had decided to make another try for the form divine. They liked her as she was.

"Where she used to accept food graciously, now she says she has too much already prepared. Well, if she has, where is she getting it? I happened to look into her canned goods closet the day she loaned me mustard. It was nearly bare."

"And I thought she was getting scrawny because I'd been roped into bringing those letters from her sister."

"We can't let her sit down there and starve," mused Mr. Lewin.

"Well, I can't force food on her," said his wife.

"Why can't you turn some of that money back to her or loan her some against it?" asked Jack.

"Someone else, but not Della," murmured Lewin. "That cabin means too much to her. She would feel we were repossessing it."

"How about Earl?"

"Doubt he had enough for himself."

"Hey," Jack jumped up, "I've got it. Hold dinner, Mother."

"If you're going down, take this."

"Not this time."

Della was sitting on her front porch rocking furiously. What a fool she'd been. Why hadn't she put in vegetables instead of flowers? How long before huckleberries and hazelnuts would be ripe? Could she borrow on her car without a tracer being sent back to Valley City?

And why, if she had to run out of money, hadn't this happened before she'd developed such an appetite?

"Hi," Jack called before he rounded the house, "maybe I'd better proposition you at a distance. I'm not good at dodging. Remember the waitress down in town?"

"Of course," Della replied wonderingly.

"She's found a man. Wants to marry him before he gets away, and can't leave the inn until she finds someone to take her shift. Of course you wouldn't consider it?"

Della remained silent for quite a long time. She had built a shell around her. She had been no farther away than the Lewin house since she'd driven in. She desperately needed that job, but she'd have to crack the shell, expose herself to the world if she took it.

"Why wouldn't I?" she asked.

"Oh, you'd go tying yourself up in knots for fear someone would recognize you. Like a criminal on the lam."

"Jack Lewin, I'll have you know I—" She saw then he was laughing at her.

"Jack, what was your real reason?"

He came closer. "Oh, I thought it an easy way for you to slip back into the human race. Early shift, six to eleven; you'll meet only natives. Five days a week; the owners take over week-ends.

"Of course you'll not be paid much—a dollar and a quarter an hour."

Swiftly Della computed. Fifty dollars less takeout. My goodness, what she could buy with that. A television for winter when the snow lay high, and food! She'd pack her cupboards until they bulged. And a few summer dresses, and of course books.

"When do I start?"

"Powder your nose and we'll go down there for dinner. The owners are up now looking for someone."

"Hurry," Della told him, afraid some other girl might squeeze in before they reached there.

She had one bad moment as they drove onto the road. Unaware of her movement, she slipped closer to Jack's side. She was remembering how she had felt the morning she had driven in, sick and shaken, wanting only a place to hide.

Now she was voluntarily leaving that place. She had eighteen dollars and thirty-six cents. When that was spent, some of it on her electric bill, she would have to return and face Lottie. This was a lesser threat.

As they drove along the twisting road, Della had a memory of something Dr. Dan had said.

"You'll find a goal somewhere along the way. When you do and feel an attack slipping up on you, you can vanquish it by concentrating upon that goal."

She had a goal. Snow came to Skyhigh when the rest of the country was washed with rain. And it remained longer. Before the first snowfall she had to have her cabin ready, with reading matter, television and radio to keep her mentally occupied, food and wood.

"Wood," she whispered, and her spirits jumped. By purchasing her winter's supply from Earl she would be helping him. Oh, she'd buy wood enough for two winters for that purpose alone.

Jack had telephoned from home. The waitress Della had met that morning a month ago and the owners were waiting.

"Well, I'll be blowed," the woman greeted her. "I wouldn'ta known you. You sure look great."

"But starved," Jack told them. "Both of us are. We didn't wait for dinner."

They chose the largest booth, and while Della hadn't the faintest idea what was placed before her she knew it was good, that she herself was at her best and that all of these people approved of her.

She had one bad moment when she presented her Social Security card, but Jack quickly covered for her. His father had talked to an associate of her physician. It would be better if Della was known to the customers as Ella or Ellie Donald. And they, respecting the older Lewin, agreed.

Halfway home, Della let out a wail of dismay. "My car—how can I change the license number?"

"Use mine," Jack offered. "I won't need it during your hours down there. You can pay for the gas, if that's what's bothering you."

They had been running the motor to keep up the batteries; now Jack proposed taking it on lonely roads after dark, and Della relaxed again. Her world was in perfect order, as long as she kept that one part of her mind closed off.

Jack, catching a glimpse of hands knotting in tension, said easily, "Why not take that thought out and give it air?"

"I can't," she replied shakily. "Not yet, I'm not ready."

"You know best; you're doing all right as you are."

But was she? Back in her cabin with her went the thought of Max. She'd never discussed him with Doctor Dan. She hadn't known he was working against her when she had made her second trip to the medical psychiatrist.

She looked around the cabin, now gay, cozy, safe, and wished she might draw the walls close to her. She wanted to hide, never to leave their security.

Restlessly she walked to the kitchen for a sedative. A cupboard door opened to find a glass for water, and an inner voice said derisively, "All right, Old Mother Hubbard. Quite a bare cupboard. How long can you hide without starving?"

What should she do?

Back went the pellet into its container, the cupboard doors were closed, and swiftly she sought the pad and pencil and swiftly wrote.

When she was through she went to bed to sleep with a tranquillity she hadn't known since she had escaped to Skyhigh.

The tinkle of her tiny travel alarm clock awakened her when sunrise was only a scarlet promise in the sky. Still she lay relaxed, aware something had happened.

The alarm? Ah, the job. She must spend part of her last money for a uniform of sorts, one she could wash out and dry overnight.

As she sat up in the chill air, her glance fell on the pad; then swiftly she went in to build a fire, put on the coffeepot, make toast.

"My you look fine as the morning," Mr. Lewin greeted her as she went to pick up Jack's car.

"I feel fine. Jack told me to air a thought I'd locked away. I did, and I learned something I'll never forget. It's too big to put into words just yet. I'll tell you later."

She was so busy trying to frame the thought she forgot she was at the wheel of a car driving out onto a public road.

She spent a wonderful morning, checking stock, even serving coffee to strangers with only a slight quiver.

Lottie also had a wonderful morning. She had discharged that horrible nurse, had herself carried downstairs, an extension put in so she had the telephone at hand. And she was using it.

Lottie was exercising her authority as estate executor. Not only Della's annuity check but Laura's was to be mailed to her home. Both girls would be there shortly to pick them up.

That will bring them to heel, she thought confidently.

Laura would come, not because she was in desperate need of the money, but because she was Laura and couldn't tolerate the thought of Lottie controlling anything that belonged to her.

Once Laura was there she, Lottie, would force news of Della's location from her, for now she knew

Laura had heard from Della. Her California agents had earned their fee insofar as they were able. Unfortunately they hadn't been able to obtain Della's address.

And, naturally, Laura hadn't confided to anyone. Her sister hadn't given her address with the letter she had written.

The big house was awesomely quiet. Of course it was the fault of that nurse, who had turned people away. Lottie tried calling a few, but those who weren't busy with graduation parties for their children were preparing for vacation.

The house was quiet, lonely. Imagine the temerity of Dr. Dan in suggesting she needed psychiatric treatment.

Dr. Dan might have argued it, but he was otherwise occupied. A young man with the gleam of desperation in his hazel eyes was seated across from him.

"It isn't often a man as young as I is given such an opportunity," Max Mayer was saying earnestly. "I want to accept, but I can't give my full attention to it until I'm sure about Della."

"Sure about what?"

He waved expressive hands. "How much damage I did to her by siding with Lottie."

"And now let's have the truth," ordered Dr. Dan, and leaned back.

"All right! I followed your suggestions. I went out with a dozen girls. Everybody and their cousin dangled them before me, begging for dates. Not one of them was anything but a bother. I've got to find out if I hate all women, Della included, because of Della. I have to see her to find out how I feel."

"Regardless of the damage it might do to her?"

"No. I'm not asking to call on her; just to see her without her seeing me. You know where she is. How about it?"

13

Dr. Dan Kendall studied the young man across
from him. He'd had occasion to check on his background. He had learned enough to understand why
friends had been eager to introduce him to unmar-
ried relations.

Max Mayer had all of the potentials for a bril-
liantly successful political career: intelligence and
charm and a deep sense of responsibility.

When his own children reached maturity, it would
be men like Mayer who would be keeping the nation
a comparatively safe place for them to live in.

Now ready to be groomed to run for his first
office, state representative, Max felt Della was a
thorn in his side. He had to resolve their relationship
before he could concentrate upon the work ahead of
him.

"When do you have your vacation?" the doctor
asked.

"That will be broken up. I'll have a few long weekends, then the first week in September."

"Good. This is the first of June. I want to do a

little checking of my own. I think I know where to locate Della. By then I'll have seen her. I'll know if it's worth the risk.

"And by then her sister should have called off her watch dogs. There will be no one following you, hoping you'll lead them to her."

"You don't think she'd ever go back to her?"

At the alarm in Mayer's voice, Dr. Dan controlled a smile. "She had many years of indoctrinations," he parried. "I doubt she'd ever return; however, I don't underestimate Mrs. Cross's power of persuasion. It wouldn't be fair to Della inadvertently to expose her before she has completely regained her health."

He advised Max to stop worrying and said the best method was to replace the worry with concentration upon his work.

"That is what Della has had to do. Be good practice for you. Any man running for or holding political office must go through a period of vilification. Start training your mind to be indifferent by replacing the outside pressure with inside strength of purpose."

"What Della has had to do," repeated Max thoughtfully. "Know something, Doctor? I'm beginning to understand why other girls bore me."

Della was far from bored at the moment. She was meeting people and not cringing from them. They were natives, at this time of the day mostly older, retired couples busy with a hobby.

"What on earth is a money tree?" she asked Hannah. "That woman skidded in and asked for cellophane tape, said she had an order of money trees going out."

"Oh, they're miniature trees, usually made from manzanita branches; their base is whatever the Kellys decide to use. Mostly they're taken to hospitals where friends tape coins to their branches.

Patients don't keep money on hand as a rule, and the coins pay for little things: cigarettes or paper, envelopes and errands. Wait; I'll show you."

She went to the back of the inn where she had sleeping quarters and returned with a little tree dangling with silver and with tiny birds. There were two owls to stand guard at night. At the base, set in moss, a trio of tiny ceramic deer seemed to browse.

Maybe, thought Della, she could find a hobby to see her through the winters; a paying hobby.

She drove home at eleven, a sense of adventure riding with her. Life need not be a complete hollow without Max. She'd fill her hours so full there wouldn't be time left to look back.

The little gray cabin was waiting but today it seemed different. It wasn't merely a haven. It was a project; something to love; something to be made as beautiful as her limited income would allow.

A week passed, and Della's vocabulary broadened. Log truckers in from delivering their first load stopped in mid-morning for a pick-up. Ham and eggs and hashed brown and stacks of toast, and were there any beans for a side dish?

Della treated her first pay check with caution, but when the second one came in she faced temptation. She wanted to window shop. Mrs. Lewin had done wonders, but she couldn't try on uniforms or happen upon bargains.

"Nor have my hair cut for me."

It was growing increasingly warm. She wanted light uniforms and short hair.

And a trip to the seaside, she thought, remembering the upper valley-to-coast highway. Suppose I do meet one of Lottie's friends. I can duck, can't I? Besides, Lottie would center her search there, not up here fifty-odd miles away.

But she must start immediately, not give the tremors a chance to catch up with her.

When she drove into the Lewins' late in the afternoon and Jack took a look at the back seat of his car, he went for the wheelbarrow.

"Isn't money wonderful?" Della cried happily as Mrs. Lewin came out. "I never had any before. I mean I never appreciated it before. Now it's fun to have. I found a second-hand store just before I got into town, and you should see what I have in the luggage carrier."

The Lewins saw and approved every item and allowed her to be alone as she took them into her cabin.

"Father, you don't feel she was risking her peace by leaving here?" Mrs. Lewin asked anxiously.

Mr. Lewin laughed. "I doubt it. Remember how she looked when she arrived? Thin, white of face but perfectly groomed. Now look down there—"

Della had come skidding up the hill on a last errand. Blue jeans, shirt with the tail hanging out on one side; a face tanned by gardening in the sun; hair a riot.

"Hey, Jack, how's for some hammer and nails?"

"Some hammer?" he teased.

"See mother," Lewin senior said complacently. "Had anyone who knew her before seen her in Seaside looking like that, she'd have been away before they recovered from shock."

Della had the Lewins down for Sunday night supper. She'd picked up some worn bamboo screens to cut off the late sun. By Sunday night they'd been painted sea-green and so had the ancient porch furniture.

"She cooks, too," Jack remarked after a first savory bite.

"He means," Della said solemnly, "I swing a mean frying pan."

"Spider," he retorted. "Hey. know how frying pans were called that? From the ones they used in fireplaces, pans with legs."

"How about skillets?"

No one gave a satisfactory answer, or cared. A full moon followed fast on the heels of the setting sun, and the valley below was filled with strange shadows, green and blue overshot with silver.

"It's perfectly silly," Della mused, as the Lewins were leaving, "but all of a sudden I'm glad my sister gave me such a bad time. I wouldn't have had this, or learned what I have learned, if I hadn't been kicked out of my downy nest.

"I think children who have no responsibility are deprived of a lot."

Mrs. Lewin put a plump arm around her to give a motherly squeeze and then joined her men.

Della remained on the porch a few moments, reliving the past weeks. The wonder of being admired and appreciated was new and, while baffling, deeply satisfying.

It was fun getting up in the morning, watching the sun announce its debut, then slowly tip over the hill to spray the roads with gold as she drove to the inn.

Monday morning was a quiet time. Della made coffee; placed bacon, eggs, fresh buns and sweet rolls where she could reach each swiftly when the log truckers returned from their first load; checked an early grocery delivery.

She was aware of some man outside, hesitant about entering. He disappeared when Jack came in for breakfast.

"This is a luxury I'm about to give up," he confessed. "With the county going on daylight saving time, mother's up before I am. Oh, well, I'll see you evenings."

After the truck had disappeared with a roar, the figure appeared again. Della felt a little apprehensive; the nearest living being across the canyon was out of call.

"So what have you learned?" she asked the girl in the mirror. "Go out and meet the threat—while you can still lock doors," she added dryly.

She went to the door and looked down just as the man turned.

"Oh, Earl, how good to see you. Come in."

Slowly he came up the steps.

"Coffee?"

Why, she wondered, hadn't he come in when Jack was there? What did he want of her?

She took him to the booth overlooking the valley and the far range, a seat where he wouldn't be seen by anyone entering. She brought coffee and heated sweet rolls, and when she was finally ready sat down to say frankly:

"You don't look as well or as peaceful as the day you delivered the wood. Wasn't that funny?" she asked. "Both of us went into a complete tizzy, each afraid of the other."

"I suppose. "He gave a half-hearted smile. "After I'd talked to Jack I woke up to what I'd done to you. Laura got away, and you were left to—"

"Now wait," Della cut in. "I wouldn't trade what happened to me for anything. Don't you see, Earl, if I hadn't caught the full impact of Lottie's consuming devotion, I wouldn't have broken away and for the rest of my life I'd have been subservient to her?"

"Then you don't think I was a heel?"

"Just a poor fish for putting up with it as long as you did. And stop blaming yourself for marrying her. You had Lottie on one side; on the other your mother who you knew was dying. And gosh, Earl, you were only a kid, weren't you?"

"Nineteen, almost twenty."

"You didn't have a Chinaman's chance. Now what brings you here besides groceries, which you usually buy when I'm not on duty?"

"Just wanted to talk to you. I'm no longer satisfied with things as they are. I feel hunted. I wanted to go to the city, and I'm afraid of getting caught. I'd like to go into tree surgery, and there again, I'm afraid.

"I thought if I talked things out with you, you could advise me."

How? Della thought frantically. For if Earl went back to face Lottie, who could guess at the lengths to which she would go to hold him?

"Earl, is there any way Lottie could hold you, legally?"

"No. I had to take one person into my general plans: an attorney. He didn't know what I proposed doing until after the news came out. He thought I had an illness, which in a sense I had, and was preparing the estate in such a way Lottie could take over with ease.

"I think he believed I contemplated suicide, because he warned me in that case the insurance wouldn't be paid. I also think he has confided in the company, and that's one reason they've held off."

Grocery customers came in to be waited on by an absent-minded Della. This problem Earl was handing her was too big for her. She must have time to consider it.

If only Max were around she could talk to him, confide in him and have him erect a legal stronghold for Earl's return to life.

"What on earth am I thinking?" she cried. And the astonished customer she inadvertently addressed muttered she didn't know; everything looked all right to her.

Morning coffee customers came in, and Earl, listening to the gay banter tossed across the counter, marveled at the change in the formerly quiet Della.

She's more like Laura now, he thought.

"Laura—" he spoke the name as Della returned— "did her marriage turn out well?"

"She seems to think so. It lasted less than a month. Moutlon thought he was marrying money, and that was one thing Laura was fresh out of. However, she seems contented."

"That first one, the fellow who broke us up," he asked. "What happened to him?"

Della flashed out a retort without thinking: "He married her sister."

"I think," Earl stood up, "I shall go down and wring Lottie's neck."

"Isn't it a little late? Besides, we can all of us blame ourselves, can't we? Your pride was hurt; not your heart. Oh, stop arguing.

"I truly believe," she sat now, staring out on the sun-drenched bowl, "that true love gives without expectation of getting. Had you truly loved Laura, or I truly loved Max, all of the Lotties in the world wouldn't have kept us apart. We'd have waited at least. We'd have given them a chance to speak for themselves, to defend themselves.

"We didn't. You jumped into marriage to Lottie, and I ran away."

That evening she repeated these words to herself. She sat on the little porch looking out on the afterglow and drew a bitter conclusion. In the last analysis one's own character determined one's destiny.

Now she could admit it was her own deep fear of any unpleasantness which had brought her under Lottie's quiet will.

Why, she thought, surprised, I'm really no different from Lottie. I was nonresisting in a negative way. Lottie used positive nonresistance. In time I might have used her weapons to gain my own way."

When Earl came in the next morning she told him a little of her feeling. "But I need time to get used to it; to apply it. Then I'll go down and see Lottie, pave the way for you. That will keep the story out of the papers and keep her from dramatizing herself."

Yet she needed help on this.

She stood looking out of the side window, considering her approach to Lottie, when she heard the door warning bell tinkle and turned to find two fishermen had come in.

"May I help you?" she parroted, walking back.

"You have," replied one. "Girl, you have! You look beautiful, wonderful. How do you feel, though I don't have to ask?"

14

DELLA waited for the nervous tremors to start, but they refused. Her curiosity was greater than her shock. These men in dark glasses with unshaven cheeks and slouch hats could be some of the private agents Lottie had sent out.

Well, if they were, she would give them a story to take back.

"Glasses," muttered one, and removed his.

The other laughed and removed his, too.

"Dr. Dan," Della cried, "the very man I want to see."

"And this is Dr. Geardon, Mr. Lewin's physician. Now tell me why you are here."

"It's all your fault," she informed him. "Your treatment brought back my appetite just as I ran out of money. Besides, Jack decided this was a good method of rejoining the human race."

"Jack?"

Dr. Geardon spoke. "Lewin's son."

"You're hungry," Della apologized. "What'll it be?"

Dr. Dan chuckled. He could envision Lottie Cross's expression had she been present.

Della took them to her favorite booth, then hurried back to prepare a mid-morning breakfast, her mind rushing right along with her fingers.

At their invitation she sat across from them, and both she and Dr. Dan thought of the last time she had sat with him.

"Please take time to visit my escape hatch, safety valve, or perhaps I should call it my incubator," she urged.

"Incubator?" both men asked.

"Umhum. That's where I cracked through the shell and came out to find an amazing world full of people like myself, with problems."

"You mentioned one as we came in, Della." Dr. Dan spoke. "It can't be serious, not when your eyes are so clear."

"It isn't mine, but it is related to me in a way."

"You wait until I've had another cup of that good coffee and then I'll leave you two alone," Geardon said.

When he did, Della plunged immediately into the problem. "There is a man here who is supposed to have died four years ago. Until he saw me he thought he was content to live out his life here."

"A man with a wife he left?" Dr. Dan asked, and his mind swept back to Max. How was he going to take this? Could it be this gay, healthy girl looked as she did because she thought she was in love, rather than, as he'd hoped, because she'd been cured of the cause of her earlier condition.

"Yes. He knows and I know she would never give him a divorce. But he wants to go into his chosen profession, to be free of the fear of detection, and he can't be until he faces her. He can't because of me.

We're afraid she might check on where he'd been hiding out."

"And you are afraid to meet her?"

"I'm not sure I'm ready," Della replied thoughtfully. "I've rationalized our relationship."

Dr. Dan started and relaxed. This girl was talking about Lottie's husband, the man supposedly killed in the plane crash.

"Go on," he urged.

She told him her findings and concluded by saying, "Knowing something is one thing; carrying it out is something else. I guess," she laughed apologetically, "I'm like an alcoholic. I've been cured, but I want to test that cure in small ways before I face a big temptation."

"Do you know why you are afraid?" he asked.

"Yes, I do. I can't out-think her. She is so subtle a person doesn't know he's trapped until the lock clicks."

"You freed yourself from that trap once," he reminded her.

"I know, and I am glad I had the experience. But frankly, Dr. Dan I don't think I could survive another try just yet. I still have a horror of that illness."

"You'll get over that," he assured her. "By the time you have to face it you'll be strong enough to walk out of any trap she can set. You have the key already: knowledge of the danger, the awareness of being in a trap. You didn't before, not consciously."

She nodded and smiled her gratitude.

He said they'd be happy to come to her cabin that evening and suggested she ask her brother-in-law to be present. And then thoughtfully he added, "You've found you pity your sister; are you aware she is a very sick woman? Mentally, I mean, and I am not saying she is crazy," he added in alarm.

The current maid at the Donovan house, the third in succession, would have questioned the doctor's qualification. To her that dame who'd just fired her was "nuts, plain nuts."

What was more, she didn't mind telling her, and for once in her quiet life Lottie slammed the door so fast the ex-employee nearly pitched down the steps.

"I don't know what's come over people," she said aloud. "A good position, good pay, and such impertinence."

She had to tell someone. She would burst if she didn't. If only Della were home so she could explain to her how kindly she had treated the girl and how miserably the creature had responded. People simply did not appreciate her goodness.

She must have an audience, though she didn't think of it in that light. She called it understanding.

She would call some friend. She went through quite a list before she found one who hadn't some emergency on hand. Even the rector had given her chapter and verse to study, as though she didn't know the Good Book from cover to cover.

"Study more than the words; study their meaning," he suggested, and went back to his duties, one hand over his receiver ear.

She tried the employment agency, but the woman there said that as girls were berry and cherry picking, with apricots only a few days away, they had no one. They received good pay and independence.

Lottie tried advertising for help in the local newspaper, but the few who answered were older women, and when she identified herself they said such things as, "With all those stairs? Not interested."

She tried the city papers, but such answers as she received were dictated on the writer's terms.

"It's all this unemployment pay, Social Security

and old age benefits supplied by us poor taxpayers."
She was down to speaking to an oil painting of her
father. "People have lost their fine independence."

"Just wait until I get my hands on that Della,"
Lottie informed the oil painting. "I can't stand this
much longer. I've a mind to sell this place and
travel."

Three weeks and many dollars later Lottie came to
a fresh decision. Della must be found. Lottie couldn't
stand this big house alone any more. She was
hemmed in by her inability to drive. Cab drivers were
discourteous; they wouldn't allow her time to shop
properly.

And the nights—the long, long nights.

She long-distanced the head of the agency, and he
said, "Mrs. Cross, I don't know what we can do that
we haven't tried."

"Try again," she ordered. "We're sure Della is
neither dead nor injured. I know her well enough to
know she wouldn't remain under cover this long.
She'll be out on the highway in that car of hers."

"Ah, the car. Do you know when her license is
due for renewal?"

"In this state, on her birthday, naturally."

"And that is?"

The fifth of September, but they send notices
earlier. If she has the money, she's the type to renew
without waiting."

"Money," murmured the agency man.

"She will have run out by now," Lottie told him.
"She must be working some place, and it would have
to be under her own name if she's using her Social
Security card. She was a private secretary."

Three things happened to Lottie in swift succession. She received a call from Max Mayer with an
order for her to release Laura Moulton's annuity
checks or face suit.

"I suppose you have Della's, too," he remarked.

"How do I know where to send them?" she defended herself. Then sadly, "If you know, I'll give them to you."

Max Mayer looked at her and read her thoughts. She would have access to the cancelled checks and starting with the point where they had been cashed, would center a search for Della.

"Della lost confidence in me the night she saw through your goodness to what lay underneath. Now don't start telling me your motivation. I know what it was: a blind, determined passion to run the lives of everyone around you.

"You may have ruined three lives and scarred a fourth."

"Three?" she gasped.

"How about your husband?" he asked, and walked away.

She broke another rule of hers: she screamed at him to get out. But he had already gone, and when she threw the first thing at hand it crashed against the closed door.

Lottie cried for an hour, then stood before her father's portrait. "But I am a good woman! you always said that, Papa. You called me your one good girl."

Someone, she decided, was lying about her. She would learn what had been said and bring defamation of character charges.

She'd call Ruth Brewer, not one of her own circle. Ruth would know what was going on, and while Ruth hadn't been friendly she wouldn't want dear Della's sister's name to be defiled.

"Are you going?" Don Brewer asked his wife.

"Yes," Ruth replied, "for Della's sake. I've heard a lot of gossip. I want to see for myself."

She saw a great deal. The lawn looked shaggy.

Untrimmed vines looped down over the old veranda; the floor was unswept.

"Isn't this place a sight?" Lottie sighed as she came to the door. "I don't know what has gotten into people these days. That gardener we've had for years just up and quit one day and for no reason at all. I've always been so considerate of him."

The interior was dark and dreary; blinds were drawn, possibly to hide the evidence of dust. The big console table in the hall no longer held a vivid flower arrangement but held instead unopened second class mail and newspapers.

"Come into Papa's study," Lottie invited her. When Ruth was seated, Lottie poured out her story. She couldn't have chosen a more unsympathetic listener.

"Yes," Ruth admitted when she was through, "I have heard things, but not gossip. What I heard were thoughtful deductions of people you had quietly manipulated into doing good works while you stood forth and took the glory.

"They felt sorry for you when your husband disappeared. They blamed Laura when she ran off. But when Della vanished on the eve of her marriage, they began to question you. What was wrong with you that those you said you loved ran away from you?"

"But," Lottie's surprise was honest, "Ruth, I've given the best I have to those three, and you know it. Why, I have lived for them."

"That's it." Ruth stood up. "You lived *for* them. They wanted a chance to live for themselves. I deliberately took Della to a psychiatrist because I could see you were squeezing the life out of her. You have a deathly embrace, Lottie."

She had reached the door when Lottie, now icy cold, caught up with her to place a question.

"No, I don't know where Della is," Ruth replied. "I don't want to know. I received a letter from her mailed in a different place from where she is living. She is happy, free and well again. She didn't give her address because she feared you would put detectives on me as you had on Laura, and she doesn't want to be found. As I said, she is living."

Lottie followed her to the porch, her lips forming a protest: "but I had only her interests at heart." She couldn't say the words. Ruth's indictment had been a deep probing scalpel.

She was still standing there when a postal car drove up. As she signed for the special delivery letter she glanced at the postmark. San Diego. She knew no one in San Diego.

Della?

"Ruth," her cry rang out triumphantly, "come here. We'll just see if Della doesn't want to come home."

Ruth waited a moment, then ran up the walk, up the steps and into the house to call a doctor. She ran back and returned to say, "Send an ambulance."

She did what she could as she waited. She picked up the letter, and when Dr. Ken roared up just ahead of the ambulance handed it to him.

"Is it from Della?" Ruth demanded.

Dr. Ken looked at her blankly, "No," he said, "it isn't," and hurried back to his car.

Dr. Ken blessed his wife above all women. There were times when a man needed to talk. He could talk to her and know that what he told her would go no further.

Lottie was all right physically, he assured her. She had had a shock and fainted. She looked as though she hadn't eaten for days; probably she was run down. That was why she had collapsed.

"The letter," he went on, "was from a man who

had recognized Earl Cross at some mountain place where he'd gone on a vacation. Earl was well and happy, living there under an assumed name.

"This chap hadn't let Earl know he'd recognized him. Now he was ready to dicker with Lottie. For a price, he would tell her where to find him."

"Isn't that using the mails or whatever?"

"He didn't put it so blatantly."

"Ken, you couldn't lose that letter, could you?"

Slowly he shook his head. "Not that I wouldn't like to. You see, Blanche, Lottie's mask slipped. Just before I left the hospital I was called back to her bedside. She asked me if there was any chance of her being bedridden."

"Chance, as in opportunity," his wife commented. "Most people would have said danger. Oh, Ken, she wouldn't. Do you realize what that would mean?"

"That's why it's better for Earl to face her soon, before she has a chance to plan any more shenanigans. Incidentally, I told her no; she was in excellent condition."

He held her at the hospital an extra day so there might be record of a thorough examination. And she, believing Dr. Ken had taken her words as a warning, waited complacently.

She could afford to wait; she needed time to plan new steps with infinite care. She would sell the Donovan house; hadn't she already proven its possibilities with that darling pink apartment?

Then she would convert everything within her control to ready cash and reinvest in such a way no one could question her right to it. There was something about controlling family finances which gave one the right to see they were dispensed to the individual's best interests and who was better able to determine that than she?

After that she would find Earl. He would have nothing. He would be happy to return to the easy life she gave those about her.

And then there was Della. Her lips straightened into a tense line. Della had turned all of her friends against her; Della was responsible for her losing her reputation as a good woman.

Della was a fine cook, and excellent nurse. Della couldn't bear to see anyone suffer, especially her beloved oldest sister.

In fancy she saw the three of them, Earl and Della and herself, established in a new home (without stairs to climb). A Christmas scene, with herself being bravely gay as she was wheeled in to see the Christmas tree spring into lighted beauty.

Della was having her Christmas in August. Like an eager child, she watched Jack install the television, climb the cabin roof to pitch the antennae.

"Just think," she caroled, "now I can choose the programs I want: comedies. I won't have to watch crime or close my eyes to it. I never could understand Lottie." She stopped. Of course. There was intricate plotting in detective plays; that was what Lottie liked.

"Tomorrow you take your car, Jack; there's no sense in you riding a pool car to that new timber stand. Besides, it's time I took another step into the world. And," she moaned, "with a new license. Mine will be due in a couple of weeks."

"You're ready?"

"Oh, yes. Besides, Earl and I and Dr. Dan will visit Lottie the first of October. I'm well now."

The two weeks passed. Lottie, carrying out her plans slowly, heard the telephone and answered it absently.

"Mrs. Cross, we've located your sister. She's a

waitress in a tavern about seventy-five miles from your home."

"A what?" cried Lottie. "She was that desperate for funds? Well!"

15

DELLA, who had greeted summer with aplomb, greeted autumn with joy. Never had she seen such a beautiful world.

Down in the vast bowl below her cabin, vine-maple lit sparks of flame that raced up the hill bringing vivid color to masses of trees previously hidden by stands of fir and hemlock.

Her larder and her wood house were full, her bookshelves stacked. She had her television set. And she had Jack.

She knew this intuitively. There were times when she feared he would say something, ask something of her she wasn't ready to answer.

Dr. Dan had told her, on his visit to her cabin, that he'd heard about Max starting a political career. He was being groomed for it by a careful study and analysis of the district his backers hoped he would represent.

She felt just a little proud. Max was the type to build foundations first. He wouldn't depend upon charm and a glib tongue to win his way. He would have as complete information on issues pending as was possible.

He'd be too busy to think of her. She'd lost her chance to explain to him. She'd charged him with perfidy without giving him a chance to defend himself.

Now she looked out on the scene, the great panorama of valley and mighty mountain, and found it smudged with grey by some distant forest fire. Soon the flames of autumn would die, grey clouds gather, and she'd be there to watch. She shivered a little.

Jack found her wrapped in a deep reverie until she heard him; then she swung to him.

"Do you intend to live up here forever?" she demanded.

"Insofar as anyone can foretell, yes. I was being groomed to follow Dad, but when I saw what business had done to him, I knew it wasn't worth it. I'd rather have fewer material possessions and more peace of mind."

She studied him. Never had he looked so handsome, his smile so indulgently tender.

"But, Jack, if all the younger men in the nation decided to do what you are doing, who would be left to keep the country safe; make it possible for men like you to live like this without fear or worry of tomorrow?"

"Maybe if we all lived this way there'd be no need of our nation or the world staying at the boiling point."

She slipped into the old rocker and considered his words. "A pastoral world. A beautiful picture, but not for our generation. At least not for all of us."

"Yet you've liked it here Della. You've won back your health and peace of mind, proven yourself capable of making your own living, of surviving economically. Would you want to return to your old life?"

"I couldn't, any more than a chicken could withdraw into its cracked shell. And I've loved every minute here. However, Jack, it was you who called it a retreat rather than an escape."

"A retreat from relationships," he corrected her gently. "After you've faced and come to an understanding with your sister, you'll be free to live anywhere without labeling it a retreat or escape."

The light grew dim, and a man crouched in a tree on the curve of the cliff folded his strong field glasses and swung them into their carrier.

He felt like a heel, spying this way, but he'd promised Dr. Dan he wouldn't approach her until the doctor told him she was ready.

He'd had a few close glimpses of her and marveled at the change. She was vivid and vibrant like the girl he'd known first in high school and later on her college vacations. And she was something more. She walked with an assurance she'd never had before.

"Come on down, Max," said a voice below.

He looked down and grabbed at the branches to keep from pitching over the cliff. "Good heavens, what are you doing here? You're not—"

"No ghost; just a brother-in-law taking over duties I ran away from four and a half years ago. Now why are you spying?"

He decided he'd better take Max to his cabin; their voices might carry. Once they were there, he satisfied himself as to Max's intentions.

"About this Jack," Max said, "what's the set-up? How does Della feel about him?"

"I don't know. I doubt if she does. Suppose you spend the night here. Tomorrow's Sunday; we'll get him up here and thrash things out.

Della awakened slowly next morning to look out

and find the grey smudge had crept over the bright autumnal foliage. It was deer season and, as there had been no recent electric storms, this meant some careless hunter had started a forest fire.

She was safe enough there; they had wide fire breaks ploughed around the Lewin land. But there were homes over in that fire area; she'd caught the glint of sunlight on windowpanes at times.

She was safe. Could anyone enjoy safety while neighbors were being driven from their homes, their security, by the arrogantly careless?

There was nothing she alone could do, but by joining others the group could fight for more protective laws and the means to enforce them.

Breakfast over, she brought autumn flowers in to brighten the cabin, watched a church service on television then after lunch changed to shirt and pedal pushers and went into her own small grove to whisper reassurance to young trees growing up between the burnt snags of once giant timber.

As she came out of the grove she noticed Mr. and Mrs. Lewin walking toward her cabin with a couple.

One look at the woman, and she stopped, her heart pounding painfully.

Lottie had found her.

She could turn and run into the woods before they saw her.

And then live in dread of the inevitable? she asked herself. "Isn't that what you did for years?"

Swallowing the fear in her throat, she walked forward easily, her keen young eyes wondering a little. Lottie seemed slightly deflated.

"Darling baby—" she had seen Della— "I've come to take you home."

Della side-stepped the embrace. "I am home, Lottie. I own this place. I love it."

"This, after the beauty and comfort I've given you?"

"Courtesy of Father. Aren't you introducing your friend, or is he the brilliant operator who finally located me?"

He smiled. "You've given us quite a chase. Well, Mrs. Cross, if you'll excuse me I'll run on; you said your sister would drive you home.

Della smiled back at him. "Her sister is home." But he hurried away.

"Della, you've changed so."

So had she, thought Della in wonder, or had she never seen her before clearly? There was a striking family resemblance, but where she was dark Lottie was fair. And she had lost considerable weight. She was thirty-five and looked fifty for some reason.

"It was about time for me to grow up, wasn't it?"

"Della, I don't like to bother you, but I haven't been well. I collapsed and was taken to the hospital. Your friend Ruth, who'd given me a truly dreadful time, poor child, didn't realize I wasn't physically able to stand it. Dr. Ken was quite concerned."

"My folks," Jack, coming around the corner spoke breathlessly, "will be glad to have you at their house. Della has but one bed. I'll bring down the wheelbarrow if you don't feel up to climbing the hill."

"Della—" there was real distress in Lottie's voice as she looked at the handsome black-haired young man, a man so strong, so sure of himself, she knew she would never be able to mold him.

"Della," she spoke as though she hadn't the strength to form words, "who is this man?"

"Her future husband if she'll have me."

They could read the intention to faint in her attitude; almost see the ignominy of being carried off in a wheelbarrow swiftly erase it. Then Jack's words came through to Della and she whirled on him.

"How nice of you to let me know," she breathed.

"Wait, just wait, until Max hears of this," cried Lottie.

Jack turned and whistled. "He knows all about it. Here, around the corner; this way," he ordered her to look toward the approaching footsteps, and it was Della who felt as Lottie had looked.

This was Max, she thought vaguely; not an apparition but a reality.

She looked at Jack and then at Max again and remembered Jack had said Max knew all about him wanting to marry her, if she'd have him. That must mean Max agreed, that he was here to formally bow out of her life.

"Young man," Lottie spoke winsomely to Jack, "would you bring me a glass of water and a chair? And, Max, I must speak to Della alone."

"About what?" he asked. "Your health?"

It was the very lead she was seeking. "Darling, I hate to bring this up when you seem so happy, but what I ask won't be for too long. I need you home to oversee nurses and maids. I've sold the big house and bought a charming cottage, but I need you.

"You see, dear, I had a dreadful shock. Earl is alive!"

Della's sudden jerk was interpreted as surprise. "Shouldn't that make you happy?"

"No, it's his poor, dear mind that was injured. I'm bringing him home, too. You love Earl, even though you don't love me."

"Where is he?" asked Della.

"I'm not sure yet. However, I've paid a man a good price to return him to me. We'll have a little time together. Darling, you don't know what I've suffered. First there was Earl, then Laura, and then you."

She had rehearsed this often in the lonely old house. She had learned by heart every gesture, every nuance. Now she went into the routine even as she watched the three who had remained. But there was something wrong, Della wasn't pitying her; she wasn't weakening, getting ready to give in to her superior wisdom.

"Oh, stow it!" Della rasped. "Go on into my cabin. I'll give you paper and pencil, an ash tray and matches. Write down what you really think, then read it. You'll want to burn it.

"I know all about your intended invalidism. You're in perfect health, but you'd make yourself ill to win us back. And we're not coming, any of us; not until you can be honest with yourself.

"You are not a good woman, Lottie. You know it or you wouldn't be forced to reiterate it. You learned when you were small that the good little girl won all of the prizes. You're still an on-the-surface good little girl who schemes to get her own way under the cover of that pseudo goodness."

"Della!"

"I'd like to love you, Lottie, but I can't. You've harmed too many people." Then wistfully she added, "I can love the idea of what you could be if you would."

Lottie heard little of what she had said; she had singled out some phrase. Eagerly she asked, "You said not any of you were coming home. I know you've written to Laura and heard from her, but what of Earl? Do you know anything?"

Max spoke for her. "He's here, Lottie. And he would like to talk to you."

Lottie wheeled on Della. "So that's why you came here, to be with my husband. You let me suffer for years and all of the time—"

"She didn't know." Jack was back with the chair and the water, but Lottie wanted neither. "They both nearly ran away when they discovered they were living on the same mountain.

"Now, Mrs. Cross, if you'll come with me I'll take you up to the summerhouse where you can talk to him in privacy."

"And," Max sighed deeply, "I'll drive you home."

It was Della who sat in the chair and accepted the water to drink it thirstily. "Max, what made me say such dreadful things to my sister?"

"Are you sorry?"

"No, I'm not, really. If someone had talked to her like that when she was small, had Father had time to realize what she was doing to herself as well as to others, neither she nor the rest of us would have had to suffer.

"Yet in a way I'm glad I did."

"Why, Della? But first let's get out of this sun."

She took him into the cabin, and he looked around and smiled. "I like this," he said. Then he sat in the comfortable lounge chair she indicated, and she tried to explain her inward growth.

"When things are too easy our mental and spiritual muscles haven't a chance to grow. I was," she smiled at him, "practically muscle-bound. And oh, how they ached as I exercised them. But, Max, I'd have been a potential Lottie had I not had this experience."

They discussed this for a while. Then, wanting to make amends for having judged him the night she had overheard him talking to Lottie, she decided to make it easier for him formally to reject her.

She told him Dr. Dan had discussed his going into politics and that she approved. When he asked why she recounted her argument with Jack.

The forest fire had dwindled now; only a thin haze hovered over the spot.

"It's like that fire. If there were no dedicated foresters, all of that wonderful basin and those mountains would be as bare as that stretch to the north once was.

"To me, men who sacrifice time, money and health in the political world are our national foresters, protecting us from national and international conflagrations insofar as they can."

And then she laughed. "I should get a soap box, and wouldn't you like some coffee?"

He nodded and followed her to the kitchenette. And she, thinking this time to cut the last threads, lightly said, "I imagine you're up here to make sure you're really free of a fiancée so you can get on with your work without worrying about me and pink apartments and marriage and that sort of thing."

"No, I've been coming up here weekends for a month, then this week for my vacation. I came because I couldn't get you out of my mind. I had to see you and make sure I was cured."

"Cured?" How flat her voice sounded.

"Of loving you. I found I wasn't. One look, and I was right back in high school when the freshman class came into the auditorium for the first time. One face, one proud little head in all that mass of giggling girls."

She'd seen just one face too, an earnest face beneath an unruly mop of black hair.

"When I finally met Jack Lewin I knew you'd escaped from more than Lottie; you'd escaped from me."

"Retreated," she corrected him softly. "I could rationalize everything else, so I tried, oh how hard I tried not to even think of you. I found I couldn't escape from love."

Jack waited impatiently and in the delay read his answer. He tried to rationalize. He didn't want a girl interested in national affairs. He wanted a wife who was peaceful, like his mother, willing to accept his way of life.

Yet for the first time he wondered if his way was wrong.

Lewin senior came out. "Let's head for the coast and get in some dawn fishing, son," he said. "Mother is putting up a lunch for us; we'll cook on the beach."

Later, when their campfire had burned to embers and they were in sleeping bags, he was to say, "What you felt wasn't love, Jack; it was a form of paternalism. Remember when you were a little fellow? You brought home every stray dog and cat that crossed your path."

"And the fawn," Jack agreed. "I remember how tough it was to turn it back to its own way of life."

He'd get over this as he had that. What he needed was some good strong interest. Maybe he was making a mistake by ignoring the fine education his parents had given him. As Della had said, if all their generation lived the pastoral life, who would be left to protect them from the greedy? A nation was only as strong as its leaders.

Lottie would have told anyone, had there been anyone to listen, that houses were peculiar. The big Donovan house had been lonely because it had so many empty rooms or was it empty memories?

But this comparatively small single-floor dwelling had that same aching hollowness.

It was understandable. She shouldn't have moved from the old neighborhood. However, all of her friends there were so busy with husbands. Well, she had a husband, and what was more, she didn't intend to let him ruin his life by a divorce.

Not that he had asked for one. He was so completely in love with that ridiculous business of his that earned him only a pittance, he didn't know there were people in the world.

Maybe she would divorce him, let the world know how brave she had been and how he had treated her.

And then not a penny of her money would he inherit if she died first. An excellent idea; she'd do it. She, Lottie Cross, would be a divorcee.

The divorce went through without protest. The newspapers confined their comments to the necessary two lines in court records.

And the house grew lonelier. Now there weren't even dreams to fill the bare corners. Maybe she should sell and move to an apartment; there she would know there were others around.

Maybe she should sell and try to invest the money. Since Laura had brought suit asking for an accounting of the estate money and had won, her poor eldest sister had had to consider her income. Della had returned her portion. She had wanted only some ridiculous things from the old Donovan house.

So she sold the house and moved to the city and for a little while reveled in bright lights and crowds and stores within easy reach.

Then the apartment grew lonely. So she had it redecorated to lighten it. Pink walls. They reminded her of something. As yes, that ridiculous Dr. Dan.

She dwelt on her memories of him. Now that she wasn't burdened with the care of loved ones, and could call a cab in a moment, she just might go in and teach him a lesson.

The more she thought of it, the more the idea appealed to her. Not that she needed psychiatric treatment. But think of the triumph she would have when he, after examination, was forced to admit she was a good woman.

Pink walls. State Representative Max Mayer and his wife of nearly a year, drove blithely to the capitol.

Della was enthusiastic about the apartment she

had found. "And they promised to have it redecorated by the time we needed occupancy," she caroled.

It was such a nice building, with tiny balconies jutting out, giving view to the silver ribbon of the Williamette running north. The rooms were large and airy and altogether delightful.

And when they wanted complete relaxation they could drive swiftly west and up that six miles to the cabin on the lip of the ledge and the warm friendship of their neighbors the Lewins.

It seemed strange that they credited Della with having inspired their son to return to his father's business, but they did and were grateful.

"Della—" Max had opened the door and stood staring first at her, then at the apartment walls, tense with apprehension.

Della Mayer looked in, blinked; then her head tipped and laughter rang out. "Max, isn't it beautiful? Like a winter afterglow. And there goes my last inhibition. It wasn't the color. It was our attitude toward it; the feeling of being trapped, forced into something not of our own choice."

They sat on the balcony that night and watched the afterglow repeat the color of the living room behind them.

"I couldn't escape from love," Della murmured thoughtfully, "but I did retreat. That was good. It gave me the time and the perspective to appreciate its wonder."

THE END